MW00647680

Tales of Dirt, Danger, and Darkness

A collection of short stories

by Paul Jay Steward

GREYHOUND PRESS

Published by Greyhound Press
8677 S State Road 243
Cloverdale IN 46120-9696
USA

First edition printed in 1998
Printed in the United States of America
McNaughton & Gunn
Saline, Michigan

The following stories originally appeared in the *Central Jersey Caver*. The newsletter of the Central New Jersey Grotto.

Library of Congress Catalog Card Number: 98-71069
ISBN 0-9663547-0-2

Acknowledgments

I would like to thank all the members of the Central New Jersey Grotto, who have given me the inspiration behind most of these stories. Also, I would like to thank the following people for their help, guidance, and answers to all my questins: John Tudek, Red Watson, Anna Watson, Emily Mobley, Michael Taylor, Steven Cohen, and Tom Rea.

Thus sayeth the Lord GOD:
. . . and those who are in strongholds and in caves
shall die by pestilence. Ezekiel-33.27

Dedication

This book is dedicated to my wife Diana, who has been asked to read these stories many, many times. And to my children, Danielle and Bryan, who have heard their mother say too many times, "Daddy will be home later, he went on a cave trip today."

Contents

Preface

I attended my first Central New Jersey Grotto meeting in December of 1991. I can still remember it quite well, all the strange looks and stares and talk of near death experiences inside caves. These people were weird, and I was going put my life in their hands while they led me on my first cave trip. When I left that cold, wet, muddy, tight New Jersey cave that day, my life would never be the same. The word CAVE would become a part of my normal vocabulary, and I would soon be looked upon as the weird one.

Early trips with the grotto were the building blocks for my stories yet to come. Stuck cavers, lost cavers, jammed locks, bat attacks, raccoons, carbide explosions, and flooded passage all helped shape my young impressionable mind. Nice easy cave trips turned into horror filled passages as my fingers typed out the trip reports. Telling the truth was much too boring for me.

In the years to come, my stories appeared in several *Speleo Digests*, adding fuel to my overactive typing fingers. But without a doubt, it was through the Caver's Digest on the internet that these stories found their way into grotto newsletters across the country. It was then that the idea of a book came to be. After reading these stories remember one thing, I really am a nice guy.

1

Confessions of a Crack Addict

I have read stories in the newspaper, and have seen it on TV, but I never thought it could happen to me. I admit now, I was a crack addict. For years crack ruled my life.

When I tried it for the first time I thought I would be stronger then the rest. Boy, was I wrong. I did my first crack with some friends. I was the only one in the group who liked it. When they found out I was still doing crack, I was cast out of the group. I was made to feel ashamed and looked down upon as a loser. I soon found new friends who did crack. They took me into their group and made me feel wanted. Next, I joined the local chapter, and then I joined the national organization. I was doing a crack a month and thought I had everything under control. I could stop anytime I wanted to; I just didn't want to. I was having too much fun and it felt so good.

After doing all of the cracks close to my home, I was forced to travel farther and farther away to find new ones that gave me the same thrill. Around this time I started doing vertical cracks. Friends and family tried talking to me at this point, telling me I didn't need to do cracks and how dangerous they were. What did they know? I could stop anytime I wanted to. Money also started to become a problem. All my equipment, gas, food, and lodging costs were putting a strain on our family budget. My wife thought I should cut back. We would argue a lot about this subject.

After a long night crack trip, I fell asleep at work. The boss found me sleeping and fired me on the spot, calling me a loser and a crack head.

When the family went on rides in the country, my face would be glued to the side window, looking for cracks. Upon seeing one, I would demand that my wife stop the car. Then I would run like a madman (as if the crack were going to disappear before I got there) to check it out. If it was a deep one, I would mark the map and come back later.

If I wasn't in a crack, I was reading about one, looking at pictures of one, or talking about one. Some mornings I woke up covered with mud, not knowing where it came from. Other times I would wake up inside a crack, not knowing how I got there or how long I had been in there. These blackouts became more and more frequent. I spent all our children's college funds and our savings on cracks. I was out of control, but didn't know it.

Regular cracks and vertical cracks didn't give me the kicks I wanted anymore. I started doing underwater cracks. These are by far the most dangerous of all cracks. At this point my wife and kids left me. I finally realized I was hooked on cracks and needed help.

After hearing of a friend's death in a water crack, I knew I had to get control of myself. I checked myself into a crack rehab, and after a month I was a new man. My wife and kids came back and I got a new job. Still, there are times when I wake up at night thinking I'm in a crack, and I even smell the moist air and feel the cool mud. I am learning to control my addiction though, and I am even able to do a commercial crack now and then. So remember, if a stranger asks you if it goes, just say, "No! Cracks can kill!"

2

The Boss of the Cave

It was Monday morning, and I had just arrived at work. I had been caving all weekend and still had visions of the trip dancing in my head. The phone was ringing as I walked into my office. It was my boss, Bill.

"Paul, do you know what time it is? You're late! Did you sleep late because you were out all weekend crawling in those holes again? You can't pay your bills by crawling in those caves you know. Now listen you mole, I want full status reports on everything you have working on the shop floor. I need written reports on everything that slipped schedule this weekend, and a recovery plan on how you are going to get back on track. I want that on my desk by 10:00 this morning. I have a meeting with the program office. Oh, and by the way, good morning loser."

Someday I'd like to take that guy into a cave and show him who is really boss. I'd get his ass stuck really good. Then I would . . . Just then my beeper went off. It was Bill again. He likes to beep me just to let me know he has me on a leash. Sometimes he beeps me in the middle of the night just to wake me up. I called him back.

"Paul, get in here right away, and bring all your reports. I have a meeting with the customer in five minutes. I need to know what our shortages are going to be this week."

"What about the other thing you called me about?"

"I don't need that until 10:00. Now get in here."

3

I went into his office. It was filled with suits and ties, not the kind of meeting I enjoy going to. He introduced me as one of those spelunker types who enjoy crawling around in the mud. They all looked at me as if I still had mud on my face from the weekend. For the next hour my boss convinced them I was the cause of all the troubles they had. The thought of getting him in a cave and teaching him a lesson carried me through that meeting and the rest of the day. It wouldn't be easy to talk him into one, but once I did the fun would start. He was the kind of boss who was your best friend outside of work but a bear at work. I'd have to wait for the right moment and then talk him into it. If I made it a challenge, I knew he would go. By Thursday he had mellowed out some, and was ripe for the picking. After our daily meeting, I threw him the bait.

"Have you ever been in a cave, Bill?"

"No! Crawling around in the mud doesn't interest me."

"It's not always muddy in there. There are lots of pretty things too. It's quite challenging, and you have to be in good physical shape. You might not be in good enough shape to go caving anyway."

"What do you mean? I'm in the best shape of my life."

"Well, it requires using muscles you don't use very often. That's what I mean."

"I can do any cave you can. Show me a cave, and we'll do it."

"Are you sure you want to do this? You're not that young anymore."

I felt badly using the age comment, but this was war. I had to make sure the hook was not coming out of this fish.

"Listen Bat Face, don't make any plans for this Saturday because we're going caving. I'll show you who's too old. Now, tell me what I need to bring."

I had victory! That was way too easy. Now I could start phase two of my plan. Saturday came very quickly. I barely had enough time to plan the evils I was to do to that man. The cave I picked was Coon Den Cave. It is a very wet cave with lots of bats, tight crawlways, thousands of cave crickets, and packs of raccoons roaming its dark passageways, waiting for the sun to go down to start their search for food. It was perfect for my plans.

I made sure to bring some rope, a jar of honey, several empty containers, and a tape player with a pre-recorded cassette. I was about an hour late for our meeting at the cave. As I pulled up in my car, he was waiting, all dressed in the clothes I told him to wear. It was 90 degrees out, and the sweat was already soaking through his clothes. He was wearing a cotton T-shirt, cotton sweat shirt, wool sweater, sneakers, and a winter jacket just as instructed. Those clothes would suck up water like a sponge.

"Where have you been, Bat Brains? I've sweated out ten pounds waiting for you."

"I got stuck in traffic. Sorry I'm late. Let's go caving."

The first hour in the cave was mostly walking passage with a few short crawls. I tried to stay about 20 feet in front of him, always making him work to try and catch up to me. He fell a few times climbing over breakdown, but nothing serious. He was actually doing fairly well for a first-time caver. He was a smoker, and I could hear him breathing heavily. I told him smoking was not allowed in caves. It was starting to make him edgy. After a short break he wanted to take the lead for a while. I let him get ahead and, as expected, he went down a wrong passage. He had asked if it was the right way. I told him I wasn't sure and to go check it out. He kept calling back, asking if he should keep crawling. I told him to keep going.

It was a wet, tight, muddy crawl that went for about 60 feet and then ended. There was no room to turn around when he reached the end. He had to crawl backwards to get out, and it took him over an hour. He was exhausted when he finally came out. I could hardly keep from laughing. He looked like he had just seen the Devil. His clothes were soaked and ripped to shreds.

"Did it go anywhere?" I asked.

He started mumbling something. I just grabbed my pack and said, "Let's go, we've got lots of cave to cover today." After that, he stayed in back and let me lead the way. I got far enough ahead of him again so he couldn't see me take a bypass to the next tight spot. When he got there, he saw me looking at him through the hole on the other side.

"Do I have to go through there?" he asked.

"I made it through, you can do it. The trick is to lie on your back with your arms at your side, push with your feet and inch your way through. Just don't slip and fall into that pit on the right. It's a 100-foot drop into water."

After several tries he finally got into the hole. It was a tube about four feet long. Just as his head came through the other side, he said he couldn't move anymore. He was stuck, just as planned. As he lay in the tube, dripping water soaked into his clothes, making his fit even tighter. The more he tried to move, the tighter he got wedged. The sharp edges of the scalloped walls were like small fingers, grabbing at him and holding him locked in place. Some of the edges cut through his clothes and into his skin. His legs stuck out one side of the tube, and his head and shoulders stuck out the other. We decided that I was to go and try to find a way around the tube and pull him out by his legs. I had to work fast or hypothermia would kill him before I had a chance to have my fun. I went through the bypass, back to the other side.

I killed some time by walking around and gathering up few things I would need. I collected a few hundred cave crickets and a bat. I surprised him on the other side by sneaking up quietly and grabbing his legs. He was not happy about that. He told me he was hearing something scurrying around. I reminded him this was Coon Den Cave, and what he was hearing was probably rabid raccoons looking for something to eat. That got him yelling all kinds of things at me.

I rolled up his pant legs, and tied the rope around both ankles. I told him to exhale, as I pulled. We tried several times with no luck, although I was not pulling very hard. I took out the tape player and turned it on. The recording of my voice spoke out to him.

"I'm going to try pulling from the other side of the pit. I think the angle will be better from there. Give me a minute while I climb over and . . . I'm slipping! I'm slipping! I can't hold on! Heeeeeelp!" I threw the tape player into the pit. My screaming voice faded into the darkness that ended in a splash.

For the next hour, he called out to me, waiting for a response that would never come. Quietly, I took the little bat out of my pack, and placed it into the bottom of his pants. I thought he was going to cause a cave-in with all his screaming and kicking, as that bat went up his leg. He finally did manage to crush it against the cave wall, but not before its sharp teeth and claws ripped his leg to shreds.

After he calmed down, I opened up the containers of cave crickets and shook them out over his legs. Most of the little buggers went up his pants. Some of them crawled over his body, through the tube, onto his face, and down his neck. His screams stopped as the crickets went into his open mouth. As he spit them out, more would go in, forcing him to keep his lips shut tight, chewing and swallowing the ones that were left in his mouth. The smaller ones found their way into his nose and up into his sinus cavities. He was left no choice but to bang his head against the rocks to squash the ones on his face and in his nose. His face became a bloody pulp and he soon knocked himself unconscious.

Next, I took out the honey and poured it all over him. At times, I saw the yellow, glowing eyes of the raccoons in my light, pacing back and forth. It was close to night outside and I knew they would be passing by soon. A good meal of honey coated flesh would be too much to resist for them. It was a shame I wouldn't get to see the raccoons having dinner, but I had to get going. I exited the cave and had a very restful sleep that night, thinking, "No more boss humiliating me." I couldn't wait until Monday.

Monday morning came, and I was busy at work when my beeper went off. I froze at the sight of the numbers flashing on my beeper. It couldn't be! It was my boss's extension! Sweat dripped from my forehead as my shaking hand dialed the number to his office. Between rings my mind raced. Maybe someone had found him after I left? Maybe the raccoons had ripped at his clothes enough to free him?

"Hello, this is Paul. Did someone page me?"

"Hello Paul, this is Frank. Could you step into Bill's office for a minute."

It was the vice-president of the company!

"Sure Frank, I'll be right there."

It was the longest walk of my life, down the hall to his office. I pictured Frank and Bill standing in there with several policemen waiting to chain me up and take me away, Bill's face wrapped in bandages, oozing blood. I opened the door slowly. To my surprise it was just Frank sitting at Bill's desk.

"Good morning Paul. Come on in and have a seat."

I sat down waiting to see Bill appear from behind the

door.

"You look really pale. Do you feel OK?"

"I think I'm getting a little cold, that's all."

"I called you in here because we haven't heard from Bill today, and we need you to fill in for him. Do you think you can do that?"

I felt the color coming back to my face.

"Yes, I'm sure I could do that."

"Good Paul, just call me if you have any trouble."

"Thanks a lot Frank. I won't let you down."

This was going to be the start of a very good Monday. Just then a cave cricket jumped across Bill's desk. Frank smashed it with his papers and said, "Those damn bugs have been all over the office today."

3

The Caver Snatchers

As a member of the Central New Jersey Grotto for three years, I have noticed that attendance is dropping significantly at meetings and trips. As the chairman for 1994, I looked into this problem to try and encourage attendance. Little did I know this project would take me to the depths of hell and back.

I started by taking the attendance records of all the meetings and trips the grotto has had in the past five years. Then, with a little calculation, I came up with the figure 43% of our members missed between 80 to 100% of all our meetings and trips. Next, I pulled the names of the 43% and checked which trips they did attend, with the hope of seeing where these people liked to go. As I read the information in front of me, a chill ran down my spine. All of these people had one thing in common. In the past five years, all had visited a little unnamed cave in West Virginia. Could they all have had an experience bad enough to stop them from caving forever?

I did some reading in the grotto library and found the location and description of the cave. It seemed like a nice cave by the description.

"After walking through this storybook entrance, one is dazzled by the rare beauty of sparkling formations of all kinds. Large walking passages make this cave easy for cavers of all sizes. Small by West Virginia standards, this 4,000-foot cave is surely the Throne Room of the Gods."

Why hadn't I heard of this cave before, and why didn't they talk about it at any meetings? The following morning I set off to West Virginia to see for myself how bad a cave this really was.

After a short hike I found a well marked trail that led to the cave. It was a large, moss-covered, walk-in entrance with a spring running down the rocks. A warm breeze which, added a strange sweet smell to the air, was blowing out from the cave. I entered cautiously, knowing I was committing the cardinal sin of caving alone.

Not far in, the walls glistened with crystals and formations dripped from the ceiling. Farther in, I realized my light was not needed anymore. A strange glow was coming from up ahead, filling the cave with an errie yellow light. Continuing deeper into the cave, I could see that the source of the light was coming from a room off one of the side passages. As I got closer to the light, the air got hotter and heavier. The sweet smell was now a nauseous odor, like that of a child getting sick from eating too much cotton candy. There was no turning back now.

As I entered the room, I was almost overcome by the heat and smell. The air was so thick that you could taste it with every breath. Instantly my clothes became soaked with a sticky film from the heavy air. The floor was covered with a thick, sticky substance about six inches deep, like bubble gum on a hot road. Was this the entrance to hell? I turned the corner and froze at the sight before me. I tried to turn and run, but my legs wouldn't work. I felt faint and almost fell into the sticky mess that covered the floor.

Cocoons, hundreds of them, as far as my light could shine. All sizes, all at different stages of development, glowing with a pulsing light, as if in rhythm to a slow beating heart. Slime oozed from the pods to form a protective coating, covering them and running down to the floor. Was this some undiscovered form of animal, one that lived in the earth and by chance entered this cave to mass produce? Was this a Martian nesting place? Was I dreaming?

The further in I went the more developed the cocoons became. I could see fluid moving through thin veins. On some, arms, legs, and heads were starting to form. I continued deeper into this chamber of horrors until the pods took on recognizable shapes.

Once again I froze at the sights before me. These were not extra-terrestrials taking over the earth, insect larvae, or even animal embryos. Here in the pods, were cavers. Some I recognized from our own grotto. Suddenly, the answers to this riddle came to me like bolts of lightning. The further along the cocoon developed, the more that caver strayed from caving.

First, they let their NSS membership lapse. Then they stopped coming to meetings. Next, they stopped paying their grotto dues, and finally they stopped caving all together. When the cocoons hatched, the form inside the pod would take over the body of the once happy caver. All association with the caving community would stop and the caver would move to Rhode Island, where there are no caves.

Who could be behind this mad scheme to stop cavers? I would have time to think about that later. Now I had to destroy this grotto from hell. For the next two days, I filled five-gallon containers with gasoline, placing them throughout then cave. Several pods were ready to hatch. I had to work fast. The smell of gasoline was too strong to enter the cave anymore. Finally, I lit a cigarette and stuck it in the thick slime of one of the gasoline soaked pods. I took one last look at the horror around me. Several cocoons wriggled as they tried to hatch. I got about a mile from the cave when the explosion rocked the ground. Looking back, I saw a huge fireball shoot out from the side of the hill. Then the entire hill disintegrated before my eyes. Was this the end, or were there other caves out there filled with more pods?

I'm not going to name the cavers I saw forming in the cocoons. I have told you the signs to look for. You know who you are. I only hope my efforts weren't too late, and the degeneration can be reversed. I will be watching attendance closely. If it does not start increasing, I will go out and find more of these caves until I've destroyed every last one.

Back home, there was a knock at the door. I opened it to see myself standing there. Slime dripped from the burnt skin onto the porch. It was time to sell my cave gear.

4

The Rise and Fall of Batman

Today, state police in Gotham City issued arrest warrants for Batman. After numerous complaints from state and local utilities, the police have been forced to seek out the Caped Crusader. He is only wanted for questioning at the present time.

One of the agencies most interested in questioning Batman is the National Speleological Society. It has been learned that the Bat Cave, rumored to be one of the largest and most beautiful caves in the area, was stripped of all formations and gutted to make room for all of Batman's equipment. Also, it is suspected that thousands of bats were gassed to death before construction began. No one has ever really seen the Bat Cave, but several local residents say a large cave did exist in the hills outside Gotham City. The whereabouts of this cave can not be confirmed.

One resident was quoted as saying he saw "truck loads of dead bats and real pretty rocks being driven out of town." Local laws do exist that forbid the destruction of cave formations and cave life.

Gotham City Gas & Electric would also like to question Batman. It is rumored the electric bill to run the Bat Cave must be in the millions by now, after all these years. The telephone company is also questioning his illegal use and hookup of the bat phone. Local police say the Batmobile is not registered in the state motor vehicle office, nor is Batman a licensed driver in any state. The FBI and the CIA want to talk to Batman concerning illegal use of computer systems and breaking into protected government files. The Nuclear Regulatory Commission would like to know where he gets the plutonium for the Batmobile's atomic batteries and how he is disposing of the spent waste. Several women say Batman is the father of their children and are demanding child support. Young Robin, Batman's most trusted companion, is suing him, stating he was required to spend most of his youth in the Bat Cave and has nightmares about all the criminals he was forced to deal with. And Alfred, Batman's butler, is in the late stages of Alzheimer's disease and must rely on state aid for health benefits. Alfred's lawyers say Batman owes him several years of back pay and Alfred is being denied unemployment benefits because he cannot verify his employment.

Is this the end of the Caped Crusader? Will Batman turn himself in, or will he join the ranks of his villains who run from the law? Stay tuned, same bat time, and same bat newspaper.

5

Lesson 1: Land Owner Relations

Paul and John drove up the long driveway in silence. They parked the car and stared at the large blue farm house in front of them. This was where the owner of Whites Indian Cave lived. It was a well known fact that Mr. White did not like cavers. They had never met Mr. White or been in his cave. This cave was one of the last on their list to check. The rumor was that this cave had over a mile of passages, and had been used by Indians and the Underground Railroad.

"Well, let's do it," John said.

They got out of the car and made the nervous walk to the front door. Meeting the owners for the first time is always hard, and meeting one that doesn't like cavers is harder yet. They knocked on the front door and waited. A dog barked from inside the house and foot steps were heard coming to the door. The door opened and there stood a large, elderly man.

"We would like to talk to Mr. White," Paul asked.

"I am Mr. White. What can I do for you?"

"My name is Paul, and this is my friend John. We're from the Central New Jersey Grotto. We are in the process of updating the database for all New Jersey caves, and verifying the locations, the land owners, and the descriptions of all the caves. We would like permission to enter your cave and survey it."

Mr. White stepped out onto the porch, and gave them

both a curious look.

"You must be mistaken. There is no cave on my property," said Mr. White.

In his most innocent voice, John said, "The name of the cave we are looking for is Whites Indian Cave. Since your name is Mr. White, we thought the cave would be on your property."

Mr. White stared at them for quite awhile after John said that. Before Mr. White could talk again, John pulled out the book *The Caves of New Jersey*. He opened to the page on Whites Indian Cave and read the description and how to find it. Finally, Mr. White spoke.

"Well, you two look like good kids. I'll be honest with you. I do own that cave, but I don't let anybody in there anymore."

"Do you mind if I ask why?" John asked.

Mr. White was quiet for a minute before he spoke again.

"I used to let cavers in that old cave all the time. Little by little, more and more cavers came. They came at all hours of the night, making noise, and always waking up me and my wife. In the morning, I would find garbage all over the place. Sometimes the gates would be left open, and the cows would get out."

As Mr. White talked, he got a far away look in his eyes. He stared up into the sky as if he were talking to the clouds. His eyes didn't blink and his words came slower as if he had just been hypnotized.

"One time cavers even broke into our house. So we finally stopped everyone from going into the cave."

The color drained from his face, and his voice got lower.

"One night we were getting ready for bed. Helen smelled the smoke first, and ran out to the barn. I looked out the window and saw the barn engulfed in flames. I called out to her as she ran into the barn to try and save the horses, but she never heard me. As I ran out to get her, the barn roof collapsed. I couldn't get near the place with all the heat. That was the last I saw of her. They never did find her body in all that mess. They said it was probably caused by one of those carbide lamps you cavers wear on your head. They found one in the ashes."

Paul and John looked at each other with a look that did not need words. Let's get the hell out of here, they thought. After hearing that story, they would rather wait until Mr. White died, and then come back and talk to the new owner.

"We're sorry to hear about your wife. We can come back another day," said Paul. "Thanks for your time."

Mr. White just stood there and stared for a while. Paul and John said good-bye and turned towards their car. When they were a few steps away Mr. White called to them.

"You two boys want to see the cave?"

They turned and looked at Mr. White. He was back to normal.

"That's not necessary. We can come back some other time," said John.

"No, no, no," said Mr. White. "Please, let me show you the cave."

He took them by the shoulders like they were his two lost sons. He walked them through his fields towards the cave. He told them that after the fire he filled in the cave, but he could open it up for them with his backhoe. He brought them to a small, filled-in sinkhole in the middle of the field.

"Well, here she is," said Mr. White. "The entrance is about 20 feet down. If you two want to come back next weekend, we'll open her up."

"You really don't have to do that, Mr. White," John said.

"No, it's about time I open that cave again, and get on

with my life. It should only take about an hour or two of digging. But listen, I don't want you guys telling anybody about this. This will be our little secret. After we open it, you can survey it and gate it. It can be your own personal cave. You can dig in it all you want, and who knows, maybe you two will find that mile of passage they say is down there."

Paul and John both thanked Mr. White as they walked back to the house.

"I'll see you two next weekend, and remember, don't tell anybody you're coming here. It's our secret."

They said their good-bye's again, and got into their car. Mr. White's words echoed in their heads. "It can be your own personal cave." All was forgotten how Mr. White went weird on them when telling the story of the fire and his wife's death. All they cared about was that they were going to open up Whites Indian Cave next weekend. Nobody had been in that cave for years. Mr. White wasn't so bad after all.

They returned the following weekend. And, as promised, they didn't tell anybody about the cave or where they were going that day. They found Mr. White already at the cave, working the backhoe. Paul and John jumped down into the sinkhole and started digging with their shovels. In a few minutes they broke through into the cave. John bent down and stuck his head into the hole. He quickly climbed out of the sinkhole and got sick. Paul and Mr. White both looked worried.

"What's wrong, John?" Paul asked

"It really stinks bad in that cave. I'm not going in there."

Mr. White laughed. "Before I sealed up the cave I threw in the dead horses from the fire. I'm sure the smell will blow out quickly."

For years the smell of the dead rotting horses was trapped in the cave. The skin and hair had long since rotted away, and all that remained now were their bones. After several minutes the smell faded. John made Paul check this time.

"It's OK," said Paul. "I'm going in."

John jumped in right behind Paul. They crawled for a short way and soon were in a tall walking passage.

"Look at all these bones," said John.

At times they couldn't see the cave floor through the bones. Hundreds of bones broke and crunched under their feet. After several hundred feet of walking passage, the ceiling became low and they had to crawl. A little farther and the cave ended.

"Well, this cave sure don't go for no mile," said Paul.

John noted to Paul that the walls looked like people had been digging with their hands.

"Why would someone dig all this with their hands?" Paul asked.

"I don't know about you, but this cave gives me the creeps," said John. "Let's survey and get out of here."

They went back to the entrance to start the survey. Suddenly they both froze. A human skull lay on the floor in front of them.

"Maybe it's from an Indian," Paul said.

As they looked around they saw more skulls. They counted five from where they were standing.

"There may be more buried under the bones on the floor too," said John.

"I don't think these are all horse bones either," Paul noted.

With that said they both ran towards the entrance. In a few minutes they were at the other end of the cave.

"Where's the entrance?" Paul yelled.

"We must have missed it," said John. "Follow me this way."

Twice they did this, back and forth from one end of the cave to the other. The entrance could not be found.

They stopped to try and calm themselves. Their heavy breathing fogged the air. In the sudden silence, they heard the last pile of dirt and stone falling on the cave entrance.

Mr. White had sealed the cave shut once again. After filling in the sinkhole Mr. White shut off the backhoe and walked over to a nearby tree. There, he opened up his pen knife and skillfully carved two more notches in the truck. There were now 12 notches. It was a tree he planted in memory of his wife. He could still remember the faces each notch represented. He smiled at a job well done. Back in the cave, Paul turned to John.

"The S.O.B. filled in the entrance! What should we do now?"

"I'll start digging in the back of the cave," spoke John.

"You go back through the cave and try and find anything we can use. I have a feeling some of those bones are from other cavers, and there might be some packs buried in there too. Look for food, water, batteries, clothes, anything that we can use. Then start digging at the entrance. Maybe one of us will get lucky."

The chill of the cave was already penetrating their bodies, and hypothermia would set in quickly. The digging would use up most of their energy. It was only a matter of time until they were dead.

Several weeks later, a small car drove up the long driveway to the blue farm house. Two young men got out of the car, walked up to the door and knocked. Mr. White opened the door.

"Hello, were from the local cave club, and we're looking for Whites Indian Cave. According to the directions in this book, it should be around here somewhere. Do you know of that cave or its whereabouts?"

"My name is Mr. White, and that cave is on my property."

The two cavers grinned from ear to ear, as if they had just found gold.

"We have been out all day, looking for that cave."

"Well, I'm sorry to disappoint you boys, but I filled it in years ago. Nobody has asked to see that cave in a long time."

"Could we at least see where the cave was?"

Seeing where the cave had been was better than finding no cave at all.

"I'll tell you what boys, I'm a bit busy now. I have a backhoe in the barn. You two come back next Saturday, and we'll open up that cave. But please, don't tell anybody you're coming here. It will be our little secret."

6

Wash Out

My dirty caving clothes stayed in a bag in the trunk of my car for the first week. I finally took the bag out and put it on the back deck of the house. A few days later animals ripped the bag open looking for food. The next day I hung the clothes on the line in the backyard. After two rain storms, the clothes blew off the line and onto the ground. It snowed the next week, so they were buried under snow for a few more days. When the snow melted, I put them back on the deck and looked at them through the kitchen door for another week. With my next caving trip only two days away, it looked like I was in danger of actually having to wash my clothes before they decomposed into dirt. So, with clothes in hand, I set out for the local laundromat to test the limits of *All Temperature Cheer.*

I pulled into the laundromat at night with my lights out. Being known as a local caver to the owners of this establishment is a dangerous thing. I sneaked in through the back door. On the far wall were wanted posters of several members from our grotto. All were banned from this laundromat over the years. I was yet to be known.

I picked a machine next to a lady who had all of her clothes hung on one of those racks on wheels. It made good cover for me while I put my clothes into the machine. I inserted my four quarters and the machine came to life.

Trying not to look guilty, I sat down and started reading the new *NSS News*. The first rinse cycle ended and I started to relax. I was almost out of here. As the next spin cycle started, I glanced up and saw the unbalance light flicker on. Just then the owner walked by. As our eyes met, I saw the look of terror in her face as she looked down and saw what I was reading. That was my first mistake.

At that point the world seemed to slow down. What took only a few seconds seemed like hours, as the horror unfolded before us. From the corner of the laundromat came a low, steady rumble in beat with the spinning of my machine. The unbalanced and overload lights were now blinking on my machine. Suddenly, bells and sirens went off and a neon sign above the machine came on flashing, "CAVING CLOTHES IN HERE!"

As the owner and I raced to fix the machine, the door of the washer flew open, spewing out a geyser of brown, slimy scum. The shaking got worse as the washer spit out my clothes one by one, as if retching from an intestinal virus. The brown scum started to glow a puke green from a glow stick I had left in my pocket. The shaking of the washer got so violent that it started a domino effect, knocking each machine over in the row. The last washer crashed through the front picture window and onto the sidewalk.

Brown and green slime was everywhere—on the ceiling and walls, on the owner and me, and on everybody's clean clothes. The change machine also got knocked over, spilling hundreds of dollars in change on the floor. A fight broke out as customers scrambled to pick up the money. A gas line also got ruptured and, as a lady was pulling apart clothes from the dryer, a static spark ignited the gas. The place blew up in a huge fireball, leaving a 15-foot hole where the laundromat used to be, killing everyone but me.

I alone must carry the burden of the death and destruction I caused that day. I hope this story will serve as a warning to all cavers contemplating taking their dirty cave clothes to the local laundromat. It could happen to you.

7

I Have Seen the Light and It Stinks

Let's see if I have this right. Carbide is a very poisonous, man-made substance. When mixed with water it creates a highly-combustible, foul-smelling gas. Carbide looks like small gray stones. These stones are placed in the bottom chamber of the lamp. The top chamber contains water that slowly drips onto the carbide. As the water dissolves the stone, a combustible gas is formed. Pressure soon builds up and the gas is forced out the tip of the lamp. The escaping gas is then ignited to form a flame that you wear on top of your head. Perhaps I was going too fast. Let's review that last sentence.

The escaping gas is then ignited to form a flame that you wear on top of your head.

Why would any intelligent person go into a cave wearing a Molotov cocktail on top of his head? The light is on, but nobody is home. Sometimes too much pressure builds up in the lamp and water bubbles out the top. Sometimes the lamp erupts into flames. Sometimes the tip gets clogged. Sometimes water drips on the flame and puts it out. Sometimes it works right. These are just a few of the problems that plague carbide cavers. As problems arise the group is usually forced to stop while the flaming caver fiddles with his lamp.

Carbide cavers can't hide. Just smell the air, and you can tell if one is close by. They say they like the smell.

They probably like the smells of fresh road kill skunk too. The smell of singed hair and burnt coveralls usually accompanies these cavers.

Nothing can quite describe the experience of being in a tight place and having a spent can of carbide dust explode in someone's pack. If carbide cavers like their lights so much, why do they use our electric light beams to see where theirs can't?

I am not a pyro-caver and never will be. Thank God for Benjamin Franklin and Thomas Edison. I'll take a light bulb any day.

8

Cave In

Two cavers stopped and stared at one another as if the answer to the question in their mind was written on each other's face. What was that noise? It was a low rumbling sound that came from deep within the cave, a sound every caver has imagined and feared. They continued in silence, a silence greater than spoken words. It was not a silence of deep thought, but one of fear. A fear that the mere mention of what they were thinking would somehow make it reality.

Again the rumble came. This time it was not only heard, but felt as well in the floor and walls of the cave. The whole cave seemed to vibrate. Dust, mud, and small stones fell from the cave's roof. Suddenly, hundreds of bats filled the passageways around them, awakened from their deep sleep by the trembling of the cave. The echoes of their beating wings filled the air. They flew in all directions, not knowing if they should face the horror of daylight or hide from the unseen terror that confronted them in their dark domain.

The rumble turned to a deafening roar and the ground around them shook violently. Huge walls of flowstone, forming since the beginning of time, exploded before their eyes. Formations of all kinds turned to dust as they fell to the floor. The lights on their helmets became useless in the thick dust-laden air. Breathing also became difficult as the rain of rock and stone continued.

Running in all directions, they stayed one step ahead of disaster as the walls collapsed around them. Soon they were driven to the cave floor by the shower of rocks pounding their bodies. Desperately, they tried to crawl through the darkness, but without the use of light, movement became impossible. They lay hugging the ground, wishing they could melt into the rock to escape the terror around them. With his face close to the ground, one caver felt a strong breeze blowing across the cave floor. Following the breeze, he found a small hole which dropped down into a lower level. Calling his friend to follow, he lowered his body into the hole.

Suddenly, another explosion rocked the cave. With no choice left, he called out to his friend one more time, and let go of the edge. Time slowed down for the caver as he fell. He lost all sensation of up or down, and a strange sense of peace came over him. This felt rather pleasant compared to the horror happening above him. He thought perhaps he had died and was on his way to heaven. A smile started to form on his face just before he hit bottom.

After being unconscious for several hours, he slowly awoke. His muscles ached, but luckily he had landed on a sandy floor and no bones had been broken. As he drifted in and out of consciousness, water would drip on his face from high above and startle him awake. Silently falling through the darkness, the drips would gain speed, stinging as they hit his face. Slowly, the water ran down his cheek to the corner of his mouth where his tongue was waiting to lick them up. His mouth was very dry from all the dust he had been breathing.

The taste of the water startled him. It seemed thicker than water, and had a taste like copper or rust. He reached up and felt the remaining water on his face. It felt slimy and sticky. He put his fingers to his nose and smelled the liquid. The smell suddenly took him back to his childhood.

He was running down the street after getting beaten up by the neighborhood bully. Blood was gushing from his broken nose and running down his throat. It was a smell he would never forget. Why would water smell like blood, he thought? He reached into his pocket and pulled out his flashlight. Relieved that it still worked, he shone the light on his hands, which were covered in red. Now he noticed his clothes were also covered with the red liquid. Was it blood? Was it his blood? Just then another drip hit the top of his head. Slowly he raised his light up, panning the walls.

He saw for the first time where he was. He had fallen into a dome pit about 40 feet in diameter. The top of the dome looked about 30 feet high. His hand froze as the light shone on an object high above his head. He began to scream. For the next several minutes his screams echoed off the walls. He thought that if he screamed loudly enough it would somehow make this whole nightmare go away. His screams stopped as his stomach retched it's contents onto the cave floor. This nocturnal playground had now turned into a den of death.

What his light had come to shine on was his friend's dead body, hanging upside-down from the hole in the ceiling. Blood dripped from the arms and the eyes were wide open, staring down at the remaining caver. His friend must have heard the shouts and tried to follow. As he crawled into the hole, falling rocks from above trapped him at his waist and crushed him to death.

The lone caver slowly recovered and checked the room for any other passages. There were none. The only way in or out of this room was through the hole his friend was blocking. He found his pack and checked its contents. He had food and water to last for several days, and enough batteries to last that long too. Taking the webbing from his pack, he made the easy climb to the top of the dome, where his friend was trapped. He was able to find a comfortable spot on a ledge. Here, he could reach out and wrap the webbing around his friend's chest several times, and then tie a tight knot. He let the rest of the webbing drop to the floor below. He had never been this close to a dead body and was surprised at how quickly it became stiff. The dripping blood had started to thicken, forming red soda straws from the fingers. And it was starting to smell in the musty spelean air.

Carefully, the caver climbed back down the wall to the bottom of the dome pit. Grabbing onto the webbing secured to his friend, he pulled lightly. Some loose rocks and dirt fell, but the body stayed stuck. He pulled harder and harder with no luck. He climbed up the webbing several feet and started to swing back and forth, trying to dislodge the body. Still, no luck. The body would pivot like the clapper of a bell, but would not break free from the rocks that encased it. All this pulling made the webbing get tighter around the dead body. Suddenly, from all the squeezing, blood and body fluids spewed out of the corpse's mouth and onto the swinging caver below. The shock of the liquid spilling onto him knocked him off the webbing and onto the cave floor.

Sand and dirt stuck to the liquids that covered the caver, turning it into a slimy, sticky, smelly mud. Rage built up in him as he tried to wipe off the mess. This was the final straw. He went to his pack, pulled out his knife, and started climbing up the cave wall again. When he reached the top, all the frustrations of the past hours were let loose as he stabbed into the cold body, cutting through skin and organs. He stopped after his arms had no more strength left in them. He rested, then started to climb down. Halfway down, he slipped on blood-soaked rocks, and fell to the cave floor. There he cried until he fell asleep.

He awoke cold and shivering from lying on the ground. He ate some food and walked around to get warm and wake up. He knew he could pull down the body now. All that held the body together was the back bone. Once the upper part of the body was removed, he could push the rest of the body through the hole and get out of this hell.

He grabbed a hold of the webbing again and pulled hard. Nothing happened. He tied a loop at the bottom and slipped his foot in to stand up. This put him a few feet above the floor. He jumped up and down on the webbing, tugging on his stuck friend. Suddenly, he was on the ground. As he looked up, he saw the webbing going limp, and his friend falling through the air. Realizing his error, he tried to move out of the way, but was too late. Falling from 30 feet up, his friend's severed body fell on top of him, knocking him out.

He awoke several minutes later. As he opened his eyes, he found himself face to face with his friend, the open eyes of the body staring at him, inches away. He screamed until he could scream no more. He rolled the body off him, and kicked it to the edge of the room. He put on his pack, and climbed up the wall once again.

All that remained was the waist and legs. He grabbed hold of the hip bones and pushed them up out of the hole. Now he was able to climb up into the hole, and crawl over the legs. He was out of the pit! He took the rocks off his friend's legs, and pushed what was left of the body through the hole back into the pit. After several hours of crawling and climbing through breakdown, he was able to find a familiar passage.

Tears came to his eyes as he saw the sunlight coming through the entrance hole. He climbed out of the cave and lay on the green grass. The air smelled good. The sky was blue. He threw all his caving gear back into the cave. He was done with caving.

9

Memoirs of a Cave Widow

I am writing this story with the hopes that some other caver's wife will see the warning signs and help her husband before it is too late.

It all started innocently enough. He went to his first grotto meeting a few years ago. The following day they took him on his first cave trip. When he came home that day he was different, never to be the same. I was to become a cave widow. In retrospect, the changes that took place in him were slow but steady.

The once-a-month cave trip turned into four or five a month. Family photos were replaced with cave pictures. Book shelves that once held great works of literature, now were packed with *NSS News*, cave books, cave maps, and cave descriptions. He would spend hours in the corner of our basement, just sitting there in the dark. One day the fire company had to rescue him from the fireplace chimney. He threw all his clothes away and would only wear overalls. Key rings were replaced with carabiners, and belts were replaced with rope. I knew it was too late when he changed his name from Kevin Carvin to Caven Cavern.

When our first girl was born, he drove us to a cave where Dr. Stone was waiting in the entrance room to deliver our child. We named her Flo, for the lovely flowstone she was born under.

He insisted we stop cleaning the house. Soon dirt was

everywhere. He also took dirt from the backyard and spread it around our house and brought bats home to roost in our attic.

His physical condition started to deteriorate. His knees were ruined from all the crawling in the caves. Light hurt his eyes, so he wore sunglasses day and night. He developed arthritis, hardening of the arteries, calcium deposits on his bones, and kidney stones. His hair fell out and gypsum crystals grew in its place. His fingernails started growing like helictites and his skin dried out and turned hard. Tears dripped from his eyes constantly and soda straws formed off his cheeks. His tongue grew into a long strip of bacon and his teeth grew into quartz crystals.

This may sound like a horror story, but it does have a happy ending. One morning, I woke to find the most beautiful formation I had ever seen in the middle of our dirty living room. I knew it was my husband. He had reached the ultimate in caving. He loved caving so much that his body refused to remain human. That day I hired a moving company to move him to his favorite cave. There he would have eternal life and be admired by his fellow cavers forever.

If your husband shows any of the signs I have described, please help him before it's too late.

10

The Alien Underground

As the car door opened, Tom Dunn was instantly reminded of the dry, searing 110-degree heat from outside. The hot air filled his lungs and dried his eyes. He was tempted to close the door, but knew the comforts of air conditioning would already be gone. Tom got out of the car and stretched his legs and back. The ride had taken longer than expected. It was already early afternoon, and he had wanted to be here hours ago. He opened up the trunk and took out his heavy pack. In it was everything he would need for the next several days. He wanted to reach the hills, which were about ten miles away, before nightfall. This was an area Tom had not explored yet. Cactus and small shrubs would make for tough travel and when the sun went down it would be cold. This is no-mans land, the middle of the New Mexico desert.

To the northwest lie the Capitan Mountains and to the south are the Guadalupe Mountains. The "Guads," as cavers called them, are home to world class caves. First there was Carlsbad Caverns, and now Lechuguilla Cave. After years of digging, Lechuguilla Cave had finally given up its secrets. That discovery in the summer of 1986 brought a gold rush of cavers to the Guads that hasn't stopped yet. An expedition into "Lech" felt the same to a caver as an Everest expedition did to a mountain climber. With all the excitement to the south, the smaller hills to the north were left unchecked.

Tom started poking around up north last year and found a few small caves. There was a big cave here somewhere. He could feel it. It was just going to take someone a little time to find it. According to the local geologists, the limestone in this area is 700 feet thick and close to the surface. Two hundred million years ago this area was a large reef under the ocean. Over time, the waters receded and the reef turned to limestone, the fundamental building block for all large caves. Finding a cave takes a lot of luck and a little skill. Knowing how to read the land and what to look for helps, but you still have to walk around and beat the bush until you find the holes.

After several hours of hiking that day, he came to a fence. It was a chain-link fence that stretched as far as the eye could see and stood ten feet tall with several rows of barbed wire across the top. Twenty feet inside stood another fence the same size, with tire tracks between the two. The inside one had small insulators on the posts, a tell-tale sign it was electrified. Beyond the two fences lay nothing but desert. If there was something in there worth fencing, it was miles away. There was a sign on the outside fence. It read: *ALL UNAUTHORIZED PERSONNEL ARE FORBIDDEN TO TRESPASS. USE OF DEADLY FORCE IS AUTHORIZED. PROPERTY OF UNITED STATES GOVERNMENT—ROSWELL AIR BASE.*

For years he had heard of this place. This was where a UFO was supposed to have crashed in the summer of 1947 and the government covered it up. The rumor was they not only recovered a ship, but several alien bodies too. The army finally came out and said it was a weather balloon. From then on, the rumors never stopped.

In a dimly lit room, a red light blinked on a large display panel, one of many that monitor for motion and sound. In this bunker, in the side of a hill, was the nerve center for security at Roswell. Every square foot of the air base was monitored very closely. A grasshopper could be detected, they said.

"Lieutenant, I have a disturbance, northeast sector. Shall I send out a chopper and check it out sir?"

"Just hold on there, Mitchell. If I remember, last week you sent out the choppers and it turned out to be a bunch of wild boars. And the week before that, it was a flock of vultures. What's it going to be this week?"

"Sir, the object is moving at three miles an hour, weighing about 160 pounds. It is still on the outer perimeter. I believe it is a person."

"Let's not be so quick to spend the tax payers' money. Do we have anybody coming in soon?"

"Yes, I have an F-117 Nighthawk on approach, 30 miles out."

"Contact him and tell him to do a low fly-by of that area."

"Yes Sir."

" Sandtrap to Omaha-Four-Niner, come in."

"This is Omaha-Four-Niner."

"We would like to redirect your approach. Steer to heading two-seven-two, and bring it down to five hundred feet. Be advised, we have a possible intrusion in the northeast sector. Turn on your forward video camera and infrared scanners, fly over that area, and then you're clear to land on seven."

"Roger, Sandtrap, camera's on. We'll be over the area in two minutes."

Two large overhead video screens came to life in the bunker. One showed the desert on a color video screen. The other showed the desert in a green tint. The lighter color greens showed a hotter surface temperature, and the darker greens a colder temperature. Footsteps could be seen in dark green, leading up to a green person.

The other video clearly showed a person walking with a backpack.

"Freeze that frame and zoom in, Mitchell."

A square appeared on the screen around the figure and then enlarged. This was done several times until the entire screen contained the image of a white male, in his mid twenties.

"Well, it's sure not wild boars or vultures this time, sir. It appears our disturbance is a hiker. He's heading north, away from us now. What would you like us to do?"

"Take that picture and scan it through the system. I want to know who he is and what he's doing out there."

It only took a few minutes for the large mainframe CRAY super computer to find the requested information. This was the one computer the government didn't want you to know about. It was able to gather information from every insurance company, library, newspaper, school, motor vehicle office, and state agency from around the world. If your name or picture was ever in print, you would be found. This was one of the pitfalls of the computer age.

"Lieutenant, we got him. His name is Thomas Dunn, age 27, lives in Dallas, Texas, and works as a machinist."

"Dallas, Texas? What's someone from Dallas walking around the middle of our desert for?"

"It says he's a member of several outdoor clubs and a caving club. Maybe he's just out hiking, like I said."

"I don't like it one bit. Send his name to the FBI, and put him on our active file. I want to know all I can about this guy, and get me an infrared scan of the area every six hours. I want to know where he goes from here."

The fence turned left, heading west. Suddenly, a black stealth plane appeared out of nowhere and flew right over Tom. He had never seen one so close. It was no wonder people around here thought they saw flying saucers, with all the experimental aircraft the Air Force was flying. As the hills became closer, the land started to change. The sand turned to dirt, trees appeared, the cactus disappeared, and the limestone became exposed. Tom found a good place to camp and settled down for the night.

The next morning Tom started hiking in a zigzag pattern across the hills. He found several small holes, but they weren't blowing any air. Large caves usually are blowing air out or sucking it in. This breathing phenomenon is caused by changes in the outside air pressure. If a hole is breathing, that's a good sign you have a large cave. After hiking most of the day with no luck, he started back to camp.

He stopped to have a bite to eat and take a rest. As he rested, he heard the sound of wind, yet felt no wind blowing. He walked toward the sound with excitement. The sound was coming from a pile of rocks at the base of a cliff a few feet away. A small breeze was coming through the rocks. He started pulling rocks away from the pile. As he rolled a large boulder, a gust of wind blew his hat off. Where the rock was, was now a large, black hole, blowing out lots of air. He picked up a small rock and threw it into the hole. It bounced several times, then there was silence for a few seconds before he heard it hit bottom. As he looked into the hole, he could not see the bottom with his light. It looked like he had found a big cave. He was too tired to enter, so he decided to spend the night by the cave and start exploring it in the morning.

Tom awoke early the next morning, still tired. It had taken a long time to fall asleep that night and he had not slept well. His mind was on that cave. He had never dropped a deep pit alone. Never cave alone and always tell someone where you are going. These are the two sacred rules of caving, and Tom was about to break both.

After a quick breakfast, he gathered his gear together. Slowly, he put on the harness, reassuring himself that everything would be all right. He had brought 200 feet of rope with him. Each knot and each piece of gear was checked and double checked. There was no room for error. He tied the rope around a tree and let the rest fall into the hole. He locked the rappel rack into the carabiner on his seat harness, fed the rope through the rack, and stepped over the edge of the pit.

Inch by inch the rope slipped through the bars of the rack, dropping him deeper and deeper into the inky blackness. It was a tight squeeze for about 20 feet and then the walls of the passage disappeared. He had entered into a massive chamber. Slowly he spun as he continued his descent. He could just make out the walls about 60 feet away. Below him was only darkness. He kept watch, waiting to see the floor appear. As he passed the 100-foot mark on the rope, the entrance light faded away. He eased up on the rope tension and his speed increased. He could hear the echo of a waterfall off in the black distance. Finally, the bottom of the pit started to come into view. He slowed his descent until his feet were on top of a large breakdown pile. Quickly, he took the rope off the rack before it had time to burn from the friction of the rappel. There were only several coils of rope left at his feet. The drop must have been about 180 feet. His first worry of not enough rope was over. He climbed down the pile of rocks, which was about 15 feet tall. At the bottom, several passages went in different directions. He entered the largest, about six feet high and ten feet wide. He checked his compass. The passage was heading north, into the hills. After several hundred feet the passage ended in a large lake room. A stream entered from the far wall. He returned to the dome room and went into another passage heading south. This passage was lower than the other, but it kept going. After a low, one-foot crawl for about 40 feet it opened up to a walking passage about ten feet high and eight feet wide. It is every caver's dream, to be in virgin cave. This discovery would surely put his name in the record books, he thought. His footsteps were the only ones to be seen in the mud and dirt. He must have walked and crawled for a another mile, when suddenly the passage ended in a cement wall!

He could not believe it. What would a cement wall be doing here, and what was on the other side? It looked rather old and was crumbling where it met the cave walls. He picked up a rock and started hitting the wall. After about 15 minutes of banging, he had exposed steel bars in the wall. He continued pounding until a large piece fell through the other side. His hand froze in mid air as light came through the hole he had just created.

"What the hell?! Lieutenant Roberts, I've got another disturbance. This one's inside the perimeter!"

"What kind of disturbance, and where's the location?"

"It's weird sir. It's just inside the northeast sector. The acoustic sensors are going nuts. It's like someone dropped out of the sky and started banging the ground."

"Where's our hiker been lately?"

"That's weird too sir. He just disappeared."

"What do you mean, he just disappeared?"

"On the last fly-by there wasn't any infrared signal. He walked into the hills and we lost him."

"Get a chopper fueled and ready to go. I want you to take me out to that area. We'll find out what's causing that disturbance, and find our hiker, too, I bet."

The engines of the AH-1 Cobra roared to life. This small, two-seat attack helicopter armed with 20-mm cannons, seven-round rocket pods, and tube launched-wire guided missiles was the "Gunship" of the Gulf War.

Captain Bill Mitchell increased the throttle and the

Cobra slowly lifted off the ground. A former helicopter pilot from the Vietnam War, Bill was right at home behind the controls. It spun around one time and then headed north across the desert with lieutenant Roberts in the co-pilot seat. In only a few minutes, they were hovering over the area of the latest disturbance.

"I don't see anything, Mitchell. Are you sure this is the area?"

"I'm positive sir. I helped put those sensors in myself. I know this area very well."

"Well, whatever was there is gone now. Let's head out to the hills, and see what we can find."

The helicopter rose up and pitched forward, taking the two men over the perimeter of the air base towards the hills to the north.

"Sir, I see a small tent off to your right."

"I see it. Hover over top of it, and give me full throttle."

The whine of the two General Electric turboshaft engines screamed to full power as the Cobra hovered over the tent. In a few seconds the tent and all its contents were blowing across the desert, ripped from its stakes by the wind of the rotor blades.

"Well, he's not in there. Start a search pattern. We'll find him."

"Sir, I really don't think we should be flying around, looking for a hiker that hasn't done anything wrong that we know of. Isn't it bad enough we just destroyed his tent?"

"You head out to his last known position, and that's an order, Mitchell! I want to find this guy and question him."

In only a matter of minutes they were over where the last known infrared signal was seen, according to their global positioning satellite. Mitchell landed the chopper in a small clearing and the two started walking around, looking for any sign of Thomas Dunn.

"Sir, I've got a pile of equipment over here, and a rope going down into a hole. Looks like our guy is a caver."

"So, that's why he disappeared. Good! We've got him cornered now. Go get your gear out of the helicopter. I want you to go down there and bring him up."

"I don't understand, sir. What has he done wrong? Why do you want to get him out? All he did was walk by our fence."

"I don't like it! Why is this guy coming all the way from Dallas to go into this hole? This cave is too close to the base."

"Sir, I can't go down there. In Vietnam I was a Tunnel Rat. I was part of a small group of men who went into underground tunnels the Viet Cong dug. There was over 200 miles of tunnels. They would ambush us, and then hide in the tunnels. It was hell down there. It was my job to go in and get them out. Once a friend tripped a bobby trap and exploded a mine in one. I was trapped for two days, with his dead body on top of me, until they dug us out. After they sent me home, it took years before I could sleep in the dark again. There's no way I could go in there now."

Lieutenant Roberts drew a gun from his side and aimed it at Mitchell. "This is a matter of national security. There's a lot more going on around here than you know of. Now you get down that hole and bring that guy out or I'll shoot you and throw your body down that hole. It's your choice."

For a few minutes Tom just stared at the light coming through the hole. A strange hospital like smell hung in the air. Finally, he got the nerve to look in, half expecting a knife or stick to be thrust through, putting out his eye. He looked quickly and then moved back. Nothing happened. He looked again. Nothing could have prepared him for the sight before him, not in his wildest dreams. It was a huge hangar. He couldn't see the far wall. Down the center of the room, he counted five disc-like aircraft. He thought at first this must be some new top-secret aircraft, until he saw them. Along the far wall were dozens of capsule-like tanks. Each housed a strange alien looking creature, floating in a green liquid. Tubes and wires were connected to each tank. Some of the creatures were moving! On the other side of the hangar were rows and rows of computers and test equipment. It looked like Mission Control. There were people everywhere. His mind raced for logical answers. Then it hit him. He must be under Roswell, and all those stories of aliens and flying saucers were true. His whole body started to shake. "I should not be seeing any of this," he thought. "People could get killed for knowing about this place." Suddenly he felt very claustrophobic, and needed to get out as quickly as possible. He grabbed a handful of mud and slapped it over the hole, gathered up his gear and headed out. It would be dark by the time he reached the entrance. He wouldn't feel comfortable until he was back home in Dallas.

After getting his gear, Captain Mitchell hooked onto the rope and started the rappel down into the cave. He heard the lieutenant's voice from above. "I'll be waiting for you, Mitchell. Don't come up without him." The deeper he went the more disoriented he became. Memories flooded his mind from the tunnels. His clothes became soaked from sweating. His heart raced and his breathing quickened. It felt like there was not enough air. Trying to hold on, his descent became quicker, as he slowly went unconscious. He finally blacked out, and free-fell the last 20 feet to the cave floor.

His body ached as he awoke. He had no idea how long he had been unconscious. He felt no bones were broken, just a few cuts and bruises. Quietly, he unhooked the rope from his harness. He cupped his hand over the flashlight and turned it on. This was the largest tunnel he had ever seen. He found a passage and crawled into it with his light out. He would find the enemy. The men in his platoon above were counting on him.

He took out his gun and held it in his left hand, pointing it ahead of him, ready to shoot. In his right hand was a long knife. Inch by inch, he slowly crawled on his knees, probing the area in front of him with the knife, searching for a buried mine or a trip wire to a booby trap. Then he froze. He heard a sound. Someone was coming toward him. "It was strange for the enemy to make so much noise," he thought. He braced himself against the wall and aimed his gun with both hands down the tunnel.

Tom moved quickly through the passages and crawlways. He was surprised at how far he had really gone. The more he thought of what he had seen, the more questions he had. He tried to focus on just getting out. He would have time to think later. As he rounded a bend he saw the muzzle flash and four loud shots rang out. The sound was deafening. The first bullet hit his helmet light and knocked him backwards. The other three missed their mark and ricocheted down the passage. Tom lay still in the mud, not moving. He could hear his heart beating as he tried to slow his breathing. The passage was smoky and smelled from the gunpowder. He could hear someone slowly coming toward him. Just lie still, he thought. He felt a hand going up his pant leg, looking for a pulse. He had fallen with his legs curled up. Just as the cold hand had stopped on a beating artery, Tom summoned up all the strength and madness within him, and kicked his legs out, aiming where the stranger's face should be. Both feet landed square into Bill's face, knocking him backwards. His head smashed against the passage wall, sending him to the ground, where he lay dazed and moaning. Tom quickly crawled back around the turn.

"Thomas Dunn, please help me."

Tom couldn't believe his ears. The guy who just tried to kill him was asking for help, and knew him by name. He remained silent as the stranger called out several times. After several minutes he called back.

"Who are you? What do you want with me?"

"Get me out of here." Moaned the voice.

"How do I know this is not a trick?"

"Here, take my gun."

Tom heard what sounded like a gun hitting the ground in front of him.

"How do I know you don't have another gun?"

"Please help me. I don't have another gun."

Tom turned on his spare light and shined it down the passage. On the ground was a man, his head lying in a pool of blood. He found the gun and slowly walked over to the stranger.

"You've got a lot of explaining to do before I help you."

"Please get me out of here. I'll tell you anything you want to know."

"Who are you? Why did you shoot at me? How do you know my name? And what's in that hangar back there?"

"My name is Bill Mitchell. I work for security at Roswell. We've been following you since you set off our sensors when you walked by the fence. I was threatened with death if I didn't come down here and get you out. I don't remember shooting you. All I remember is, I was going down the pit and I blacked out, and then I woke up here. As far as some hangar back there, I don't know what you're talking about."

Tom sat down and showed Bill where he had shot his light out, and told him all he saw through the hole in the wall. Bill sat wide-eyed in disbelief.

"I've worked here for ten years. I can't believe something like that was right under my feet."

"It's there. Believe me! Who is in charge of security there?"

"Lieutenant Roberts is. The old lieutenant was killed in a car accident. He was replaced by Roberts a few months ago."

"And he threatened you with death if you wouldn't get me out?"

"Yep, he did mention something about national security, but with a gun pointed at me, I wasn't listening to all he was saying."

"Well, let's get you out of here. I think we should have a talk with the lieutenant."

"He'll be waiting for us at the entrance. You can count on that."

It took over two hours for the two to get back to the pit. Bill had lost a lot of blood, and had to be helped most of the way. At the pit, Tom rigged Bill up with his extra rope walker. This was a system that worked with small cams. It allowed someone to slide up a rope without sliding down. Bill went first, so Tom could help push him up the rope. It was slow going, but within an hour they were both out of the pit.

Quietly, they unhooked from the rope. Tom looked up toward the sky. Orion was just rising in the south. The sky would never look the same, he thought. They were up there somewhere. He knew it now.

"Bill, you stay here. I'll go get your lieutenant. He can help us get you into the chopper."

Tom walked toward the chopper. There was a light on inside it, and he could see someone sleeping in the seat. He knocked on the door. Roberts was startled awake, with gun in hand.

"My name is Tom Dunn, but I believe you

already know that. Your friend Bill is over by the cave. He had a fall. He's hurt pretty badly, and we need your help."

"Just hold it right there!"

"You don't need to point that gun at me. I'm unarmed. I'll tell you all you want, but now I think we should get your friend to a hospital."

"I said, hold it right there! What were you doing in that cave?"

"Just exploring. It's what all cavers do."

"Did you see anything strange down there?"

Tom tried to lie, but his eyes gave him away. "Just the usual stuff in caves."

"Come on," said lieutenant Roberts. "Let's go see our hurt friend."

Tom was pushed with a pistol in the middle of his back. When they reached the pit, Bill was nowhere to be seen.

"Well, where is he?"

"He was here a minute ago, I swear!"

Roberts took a few steps back and aimed his gun at Tom.

"You know what I think? I think you killed him in that cave. I don't think he was ever here."

"That's not true. I probably saved his life. I helped him out. He was here. He's got to be around here somewhere. Start looking around. We'll find him. He couldn't have gotten too far."

The lieutenant raised his gun to the level of Tom's chest. "It's a shame you tried to resist, when we just wanted to ask you a few questions."

Just then the explosive roar of the 20mm guns from the helicopter broke the night. A hideous unearthly scream pierced Tom's ears. The ground around him exploded with bullets as he dove for cover. When the roar was over Tom raised his head. Bill Mitchell slowly got out of the helicopter, and walked over to join Tom. In the light of Tom's flashlight they saw yellow slime oozing from what was left of the lieutenant's body, as he changed from human back to his alien form.

"How did you know?"

"I didn't know he was a freaking alien! I thought if he threatened to kill me, he may want to kill you."

Tom looked at Bill with fear in his eyes.

"Don't look at me like that. I'm not one of them. My blood's red. Let's get the hell out of here! Get in the chopper. I'll fly us back to base."

"Are you OK to fly that thing?"

"I've flown these things with more than a cut on my head. Get in."

"I don't think it's a good idea to go back to the base. What if more of those things are there too? There's only one thing I think we should do. Fly to the nearest airport. We need to talk to someone in Washington as soon as possible.

As Bill started the helicopter, Tom picked up the alien head and placed it in the helicopter.

"Get that thing out of here!" Bill screamed.

"If you want anybody to believe us, we better have proof."

"Well, cover it up with something. It stinks too!"

The helicopter rose into the air. They flew across the desert at top speed and stayed low to the ground to avoid any radar.

Several weeks later at his home in Dallas, Tom was sitting down to watch some TV when a news report broke across the screen.

"World leaders are up in arms today. It was announced that the United States has started underground nuclear testing again, breaking the nuclear test ban treaty it signed ten years ago. The site of the recent underground test was Roswell Air Base in New Mexico. The President is standing firm on his decision stating, "The test was needed to help in the development of space-based, nuclear-powered laser weapons."

The newsman continued, "As you remember years ago, Roswell Air Base was once the site of numerous rumors concerning crashed alien spacecraft that the government . . ."

Tom turned the TV to another channel.

11

Diary of a Carbide Caver

This Diary was found outside a cave in eastern Pennsylvania. The author is unknown.

9:00 A.M. As I was filling my lamp with carbide, I dropped the lamp and all the carbide fell out onto the ground, had to refill lamp.

10:00 A.M. Drank all my water on the hike to the cave, had to borrow water from another caver to fill my lamp.

10:10 A.M. While filling the lamp, I spilled the water all over my arm and pants.

10:12 A.M. Striker broke off as I was trying to light lamp, had to use another lamp to light mine.

10:15 A.M. Lamp is lit, we enter cave.

10:20 A.M. Water starts bubbling out of the lamp and it erupts into flames. Have to replace wet felt. Need someone to light my lamp, striker is still broken.

10:30 A.M. Caving again.

10:50 A.M. Lamp goes out. Tip is clogged. While cleaning tip with a tip cleaner it breaks inside the tip. Need to replace with new tip. Electric caver gives me his lighter to light my lamp.

11:00 A.M. Lamp is acting funny, must be old carbide.

11:30 A.M. Stop and clean mud from reflector. Burn hand. Have a large burn blister.

11:45 A.M. Caving with bandaged hand.

12:00 P.M. Flame is low, need a carbide change. Need electric caver to shine light on me while I change carbide.

12:10 P.M. Caving again.

12:20 P.M. Lamp is leaking water. Have pinhole in base of lamp. Seal hole with chewing gum from electric caver.

12:25 P.M. Caving again.

12:30 P.M. Lamp is leaking gas. Smell makes me sick and I puke on another carbide caver and put his lamp out.

12:45 P.M. Clean up mess, caving again.

1:05 P.M. Used carbide in pack explodes, many cavers mess pants.

1:20 P.M. Caving again, group makes me stay in the back.

1:30 P.M. Burned caver's leg in front of me in a tight crawl. He kicks me in the face, and puts my light out. Right eye is swollen shut. Need help to re-light lamp. Have one good hand and eye left.

1:40 P.M. Still smell gas. Use more gum to seal around

the threads.

1:50 P.M. Large bubble forms in gum from the escaping gas and pops. Covers my lamp and my one good eye with a thin layer of gum. Electric caver takes my lamp and throws it into a deep pit. Other cavers help me out of the cave. On the way home I will stop and buy an electric caving light.

After reading this diary I ask myself, why would anybody use a carbide lamp? Perhaps we should add this question to the many that have plagued modern man.

Why are there no plums in plum pudding?
Why do we park on the driveway and drive on the parkway?
Why are some raincoats dry clean only?
Why is it called rush hour when we are stopped in traffic?
Why do hot-dogs come ten to a pack and rolls come eight to a pack?
What is the difference between a boat and a ship?
Where does all the rubber go from our tires?
Why call it Rhode Island if it's not an island?
Why do cavers use carbide?

12

Photo Opportunity

"Paul, I found it! Over here, hurry!"

Paul heard Dan's voice calling, echoing down the valley. They had been hiking all day on Cave Mountain, looking for the elusive Hot Air Cave. For months the two had been coming up here to look for this cave. Over the years, descriptions of the cave put it at seven different locations on the mountain. Some said it was close to the summit, others said it was down by the valley. Some said the north side, some said the east. No one had found it for the past three years. Paul and Dan had made it their mission to find it, even if it killed them. In the coldest winter weather or the hottest summer, they would be out there looking for that cave. After a short hike, Paul joined his friend standing next to a large, dark opening.

"Well, you sure did find a cave. Do you think it's Warm Air Cave?"

"Hell yea it's Warm Air Cave! Go stand by the entrance. We finally found it!"

It was an entrance about five feet high and eight feet wide. Paul walked up to the entrance and felt the warm air blowing out.

"This is amazing! How could anybody miss this? I was starting to think this cave was only a myth. Where do you think the warm air comes from, and what's that smell? It smells like someone's bad breath!"

"We'll find out soon. Maybe from a thermal vent or a

hot spring. Let's get our gear on and check it out."

As Dan was getting dressed, Paul was getting his camera out.

"Come on Paul, get dressed."

"I will, but first I want to get a picture of us in front of the entrance. I'll put the camera on this rock and set the timer, then I'll run and stand next to you. When it stops beeping, smile."

Dan stood by the opening waiting for Paul, who was fiddling with his camera.

"Paul, will you hurry up. I hear something behind me."

"Just hold your pants on. I want this to be good."

"I'm not kidding. Something is moving around in there. Hurry up!"

"It's probably a raccoon or something. Just be patient, I'm almost done."

"There's something big in there, and it's getting closer. WILL YOU HURRY!"

Paul took one last look into the camera view finder. Dan was gone!

"Dan will you come out of there so I can take this picture. I'm ready now! Don't make me come in there and get you. Will you come on out?"

There was no answer. Paul walked up the mud covered slope. Dan's footprints stopped at the entrance.

"Where did he get to?" thought Paul.

Paul returned to his pack, got his helmet and light out, and went into the cave. He was surprised at how small it really was. The cave went back about 50 feet and stopped. There were no side passages anywhere. The warm air had stopped blowing, and that awful smell was gone too. In the back of the cave was Dan's carbide lamp, lying in a pool of yellow, sticky slime. Paul went outside and called up and down the mountain for his friend until his throat hurt. He sat by the cave for the next several hours, hoping for his friend to return. As the sun was setting, Paul started down the mountain, carrying both their gear.

If only Paul had turned around on his way down, he would have seen the cave closing up, leaving no trace of it ever having been there, only to open again at another time and place on the mountain, and wait for its next meal.

The next day's newspaper read: Another person mysteriously disappears on Cave Mountain.

13

Bat Tales

Winter is finally here. I've been looking forward to this year's hibernation all summer long. I can remember in my younger days staying up all night and half the morning chasing bugs. Sometimes I even skipped some of my hibernation time. Now, I get so tired at night I can't even make it until sunrise. My echolocation isn't as good as it use to be either. I used to be able to find a mosquito at 50 feet. Now I have trouble finding a moth at ten. Well, it's nothing a few month's sleep won't cure. I just hate hanging upside down for so long. All the blood goes to my head and my feet get so cold and tired hanging onto the rocks. Maybe next winter I'll go visit my brother in Mexico. He thinks I'm nuts spending the winter in New Jersey. At least I don't have to sleep with all those vampire bats.

My echolocation is picking up a large group of cavers coming this way. Oh no! It's another group of beginner cavers, being led by that guy Paul Steward. Who does he think he is, Floyd Collins? Here they come. Why did I pick the prettiest formation to sleep next to? Now I have eight bright lights blinding me. Don't they know I'm trying to get some sleep?

Hey! Watch that carbide light, buddy! I hope they don't try and touch me. I've heard you can get rabies from cavers. Maybe I'll drop some guano in their eyes. That will teach them not to bother me. I can see I'm not going to get any sleep today. I'll have a little fun, and fly around their heads a few times and scare them. I love to see them run for cover when I do that. Who do they think I am, Count Dracula?

Good, they're going now. I'll go find another place to rest until they're gone for good. These cavers are nuts, squeezing through tight holes, crawling through mud and water, and climbing over rocks. Being a bat doesn't seem so bad after watching these guys.

I'll make you a deal, Paul, if you don't bring any more cavers in here this winter, I won't follow you home and scare your kids. The cave will smell of humans for a couple of days, but at least I can get some sleep now. Maybe I'll dream of flying through locust-filled fields with my mouth open, or wiping out the entire gypsy moth population by myself. I feel my heart beat slowing down, and my body getting numb. I'm going into hibernation! I hope water doesn't drip on me and turn me into a formation by springtime.

14

Rules Are Rules

It says in the grotto's constitution that, "Members may be permanently suspended from the grotto for conduct unbecoming to the NSS, the grotto, or the caving community."

I am writing this letter to report that I have noticed blatant disregard for this rule. I have seen fellow cavers engaged in conversation with surface people. Given the growing number of surface dwellers, I can understand a chance meeting once in a while. However, to associate and mingle with these people is a speleocrime of the highest order. These people do not understand our need to be underground. They will try to talk you out of caving. They will make you feel unwanted and look at you as the filth of the earth. They are to be avoided at all cost.

I have also noticed many members with dark tans this summer. Real cavers do not lie out on the beach and worship the sun. They avoid direct light and seek the darkness whenever possible.

Also, many "true cavers" have very clean rug mats in their cars. This is impossible for a true caver.

Real cavers are allowed to have only one pair of good jeans. The rest must be ripped and stained and never thrown out. They must also wear a caving T-shirt to grotto meetings.

On a recent cave trip, I saw a so called "Joe Caver"

afraid of a bat! Cavers are not afraid of bats. The bat is the sacred symbol of the underworld. A caver afraid of a bat is like an auto mechanic afraid of oil.

I think I have said enough for now. You know who you are, and the rules you are breaking. If these crimes continue, I will be forced to take action. Let's try to change our ways before it is too late.

15

The Great Debate

Part one

The night arrived for the great carbide debate. Paul "the anti-carbide caver" Steward and Ralph "I love the smell of carbide in the morning" Johnson met in the doorway to Theresa Lewis's house. They locked eyes, and exchanged a firm hand shake. Each knew this would be a fight to the finish.

The arena was set in Theresa's living room, leaving standing room only for anyone arriving late. Ralph started the debate with general questions to all, finding out that only a small portion of those present were carbide cavers. Paul smiled as the hands went up for those who used electric lights. Ralph now knew he faced an angry mob of electric cavers, wishing to take vengeance on him for all the carbide gas they had been forced to breathe over the years.

Ralph brought a secret weapon with him for this debate, Buzz Rudderow. Buzz was past chairman of the grotto for many years, former electric caver gone carbide, and all around nice guy. His opinion would rank high among many. Together Ralph and Buzz would form a strong defense for the carbide caver.

On Paul's team was Gene Russo. Both Paul and Gene had strong opinions on the use of carbide and electric. They too would form a strong pair, leaving no stone unturned in the fight for the electric caver.

For the next hour both sides battled it out. Ralph

continually blamed the caver, not the lamp for most of its troubles, while Paul stuck to the better safety aspects of using electric. In the end, both sides did agree on several things. Paul and Gene agreed the carbide lamp does throw a better light at close range, and would be more dependable on extended cave trips of several days. Ralph and Buzz agreed many cavers do not use their lamps properly, and a carbide lamp should come with a book instructing the proper use and maintenance. Also, an electric light is better for seeing farther ahead of you.

Part Two

Long after Ralph and most of the others went home that night, several of us stayed to talk. Suddenly, my eyes froze on an object across the room. Drawn like Moses to the burning bush, I slowly walked over and picked it up. I examined the object closely. It felt like I had found the broom stick of the Wicked Witch of the West.

Like a hunter displaying his kill, I held the object high above my head for all present to see. A hush fell upon the room as all eyes stared at the object in my raised hands. Everybody in the room dropped to their knees and feared to look at me. There in my raised hands I held Ralph's most prized possession, his favorite 15-year-old carbide lamp.

This was not just another lamp, but an extension of Ralph's soul, his meaning for life, his Holy Grail. How ironic it was for me, "the anti-carbide caver" to come into possession of Ralph's carbide lamp. Was this an omen of some sort? I left that night with the lamp tucked deep in my bag, and my mind filled with thoughts of my children's college fund.

Later that night, Theresa received a call from Ralph concerned about the whereabouts of his lamp. She told him I had the lamp. With that said, Ralph dropped the phone moaning, "no, no, say it isn't so."

I called Ralph several days later, confirming his worst fears. I told him I wanted $1,000 in small unmarked bills, and not to call the police or his lamp would be history. He was also to stay by the phone and he would be contacted for further details. He told me he would comply with my wishes, and warned me to be very careful with the lamp. He said the lamp was haunted by demons from the underworld, and bad things would happen to those who would bring harm to it. I hung up the phone laughing at the thought of Ralph believing his lamp is possessed by demons. Sure he would get his lamp back, but not before I converted it to electric.

I removed the burner tip, and a bulb fit very nicely in its place. Next I removed the stem that went down into the bowl. A D-cell battery could now be put into the bottom bowl with the top screwed on. I ran wires from the battery to the bulb, and installed a micro switch on top of the lamp.

I turned on the new "electric carbide lamp" and was surprised at the light it gave off. It had a carbide lamp glow, with a bright spot in the middle. This was the perfect light for caving. Did I just invent a new light? I would have to try it out in a cave to be sure.

I tried to turn off the lamp, but it wouldn't work. The light seemed to get brighter. It also got so hot that I could not hold it in my hands any longer. I dropped the lamp, and thick white smoke started coming from it, filling the room. I thought it was going to explode. The smoke started to circle around the room like a tornado, forming a funnel from the lamp. Deep inside the smoke I could see the image of something starting to form.

The echoes of Ralph's warning hit me like lightning bolts. "The lamp is haunted by demons from the underworld." What had I done? I closed my eyes. When I opened them again, I knew it was no dream.

The smoke had cleared, and standing before me was the image of Elvis. This was not the Elvis we had all come to know and love, dressed in white flashy clothes. This one had flesh dripping from exposed bone, worms crawling in his eye sockets, and guts hanging out from one side where skin and muscle once were. The dripping flesh burned like acid as it hit the floor. Through the exposed ribs, I could see his lungs expand with air as he breathed. I was almost overcome from the heat and smell from his breath.

As he started to talk, teeth fell out from his rotting gums. His voice sounded like a record being played on slow speed. I realized he was not trying to talk, but was singing the song, "Hound Dog." At one point during the song his tongue fell out of his mouth and dissolved into a pool of slime. After the song was over, the image of Elvis turned into that of Ralph Johnson!

Slowly, he walked toward me laughing hysterically. In his mouth was a carbide lamp shooting a long flame out at me. He said, "Let's have a debate now, Paul." At the end of each of his fingers was a small flame. I realized he was a walking carbide lamp! Suddenly, I had an idea. I ran and found my electric caving light, turned it on, and adjusted the zoom to a narrow beam. I aimed the bright light into his eyes. Like a vampire seeing a cross, he covered his eyes and backed off. Then I found my bag of used batteries and started throwing them at him. Each battery worked like a bullet as it hit him, putting large holes where flesh once was.

Ralph reached into his pocket and pulled out a handful of carbide, shoving it into his mouth and swallowing. The flames in his hands and mouth grew brighter. He came at me again, but I had one last trick up my sleeve. I opened a bottle of vinegar and started pouring it all over him and down his throat. The carbide in him mixed with the vinegar and started to foam. He fell to the floor, and slowly started to dissolve, like a salted slug.

I didn't know how many more demons would appear from the lamp, and I was all out of vinegar. So I quickly put the lamp back to the way it was and hoped that it would work properly. I wasn't sure if I had really killed Ralph or just a demon that looked like him.

I dialed Ralph's phone and he picked it up on the first ring, still waiting by the phone as requested. He told me he had collected the $1,000 for his lamp. I told him the deal was off and to come over right now or I would run over his lamp with my car. One hour later, Ralph was knocking on my door.

I opened the door just enough to get my arm out to hand him his lamp. I could not bear to look into his eyes for fear of seeing the demon. As he walked away, I thought I heard him humming the song, "Hound Dog."

I don't think I'll be buying a carbide lamp anytime soon. You may not believe it, but this story really did happen. I have seen the evil that lurks inside carbide lamps!

16

Animal

Deep within the darkness of the cave the animal awoke. He lay still for a while as his senses adjusted, wondering what had awoken him this time. Was it a smell, a sound, a small tremor from deep within the earth, or was it one of those strange dreams he would have from time to time?

In those dreams he would see other animals of all different shapes and sizes walking across beautiful lands. He went to the entrance of the cave and sat down. He could feel a cool breeze, yet he saw nothing. Evolution had stolen his sight. After hundreds of years of darkness, his eyes were no longer needed. A large nose covered most of his face. Where eyes once were, he now had two small indentations. Large ears grew from the sides of his head. He had a small mouth without any teeth. Although he had no sight, his sense of touch, smell, and hearing were very sensitive. Thick, tough skin covered his entire body. At the end of each of his four legs he had five very long fingers for feeling around in the darkness. All he lived on was water seeping into the cave and the bacteria that it carried.

As he sat at the entrance, he sensed a vast land before him. To venture out into that land would surely mean his death. This cave was not only his home, but his prison. He had no idea how long he had lived in this cave or how he came to be here. In all his time in the cave, he never sensed the presence of another. He would spend hours near the entrance, hoping to smell or hear another animal. The truth was, he was the last. Not only the last of his breed, but the last of any breed. The last surviving animal on the face of the earth, driven into a cave for some unknown reason and forced to evolve into some hideous form of life to survive.

The animal got up and went back into the depths of the cave. He found his favorite room and went back to sleep. Again, he dreamed of wondrous lands with green trees stretching across the horizon. Herds of animals roamed the lands. This dream was different from the others. Instead of watching the animals, he now was one of them. One of the two-legged kind that walked erect. He was with a group, climbing a cliff face to reach the entrance of a cave. They called themselves cavers.

Suddenly, across the land, huge mushroom clouds appeared everywhere along the horizon. High on the cliff face with nowhere to go, the cavers ran to the shelter of the cave. For several minutes the cave was illuminated by a bright white light as the group ran deeper into the cave. The light was followed by strong winds that tossed the cavers about. Within days, thick dark clouds would cover the earth, drowning it in a darkness that would last for centuries.

The animal awoke panting from the dream still fresh in his mind. He now understood. These were not dreams but small bits of memory that had survived the evolutionary process locked deep inside his mind. He now had the answers to all his questions. Feeling a deep sadness, he went back to sleep.

17

Things to Talk About at Grotto Meetings

Let's talk about a few of the things that don't get brought up at most grotto meetings. How about if we start with underwear. I'm not talking about what style you wear, I'm talking about the color of them. If you are a true caver then somewhere in your dresser is a nice pair of white underwear that has brown mud streaks permanently stained on the backside. These are not the kind that you hang out on the line to dry with the rest of your caving clothes. They get to dry hanging over the tub. Who cares if the neighbors see your dirty overalls, just don't let them see those brown stained underwear. I guess bras would fall into this same category too. I wouldn't know. I've never seen bras hanging on any caver's clothes line either.

Now, let's talk about farting. Everybody does it, and it's a natural bodily function, but do you have to do it in the tightest crawlway of the cave? You woke up early, and you've been on the road for three hours. You had a greasy breakfast with five cups of coffee, and this is now mixed with the beer and junk food from the grotto meeting the night before. While all this food is fermenting in your stomach, you start crawling through a cave, squeezing your insides around. Silently, the mother of all smells soon fills the passage that you're in. With no escape in sight, you are forced to breathe in the smell of your friend's rotting stomach. This is not a smell that goes away quickly. This is one that lingers for hours, hanging in the air like a thick fog, sticking to anything that passes by. A cave is not the place for a fart war. Don't start one.

How about the subject of survival. I don't mean eating candy bars and licking stalagmites for two days until somebody finds you. I'm talking about the ultimate in survival. Let me set the scene:

You're underground in a huge cave system, miles from the entrance. Suddenly, a small underground tremor collapses the passages around you, and your friend gets killed by falling rocks. You are now trapped in a small room with your dead friend, and without any food or water. Days pass by and you grow weaker and weaker from lack of food and water. Finally, you are left no choice. In order to sustain your life you must find something to eat or you will die. You are now forced into the ultimate in survival, the consumption of human flesh to save your life.

Where do you start, an arm, a leg, a rib? If your friend was good looking would that make the taste seem better? Do you leave the skin on or do you peel it off? Do you cut it in long strips or small chunks? Should you cut and eat it right away or do you let it dry out like beef jerky? Will it taste like chicken? Perhaps you should ask yourself these questions before you go caving again. The people you go caving with might just save your life.

How about the use of caves for things other than caving? If one wanted to hide a large sum of money a large cave system would be just the place. Dig a hole, drop the money in, cover it with a little mud, and it's hidden. Come to think of it, you could hide a body quite well in a cave too. If you were ever going to kidnap someone a cave would be a great place to keep the person. Just bring him to a small room in a large cave and leave him there without any light. I'm sure not many FBI agents are cavers.

18

Cave's Revenge

The two teenage boys entered the cave filled with nervous excitement. They had just found the cave several hours ago and had raced home to get flashlights and provisions. Each boy had an empty pack, a hammer, and extra batteries. Their plan was simple. Take only the best and biggest rocks they could find. They would start from the back of the cave and work to the entrance. This way they would not have to carry extra weight on the way in.

As they wandered through the cave they yelled and shouted to one another comparing the rocks they found, trying to outdo each other in size and beauty. They wandered for hours, amazed at the underground world they had discovered. With no end to the cave in sight they stopped. This would be as far as they would go today.

Excitedly, they took out their hammers and went to work. Some formations only took a small tap while others needed many hits with their hammers to break them loose. These rocks were sure to make them the most popular kids in school. While they worked, they discussed which of their friends would receive which rocks. Their small packs filled quickly, so they began dropping what they had for better ones. Behind them the passages became littered with destroyed formations of every kind.

They found small pools of pure white cave pearls.

Taking these pretty white stones, they skimmed them across a shallow pond, breaking the fragile rimstone dams on the other side. Some they threw high across the ceiling, breaking hundreds of hanging sodastraws at a time. It looked like it was snowing in the cave as the long formations fell to the cave floor.

One of them urinated in a small pool. Shortly thereafter some blind fish were floating on the surface of the water, dead. Another time one of the boys yelled to the other, "look, bat kebobs" as he held up several bats skewered on a long sharp stalactite, still moving as the last ounce of life drained from their small bodies.

From deep within the cave came a low noise, like that of a man in pain. The noise came from every dark corner of the cave. The two kids froze in fear as the sound echoed off the cave walls. They ran in all directions, trying to find the way out. Each thought the other knew the way. In their running around, they got separated. Slowly, their shouts to one another became more and more distant until they both were lost. It was now the cave's turn to have some fun.

The boy who had killed the bats rested. In the silence of the cave came a noise, like a train you hear off in the distance. The boy sat frozen. Suddenly, thousands of bats filled the room and flew around his head. Some went in his hair and down his shirt, while others bit his face and arms. They ripped his clothes and chewed at his flesh. He had hundreds of bites over his body.

As suddenly as the bats appeared they were gone. As he lay on the cave floor trying to wish this into a bad dream his light caught movement on the walls. His eyes went wide in horror, as he saw millions of cave crickets and spiders covering every inch of the walls, floor, and ceiling. In seconds he was covered with the bugs, nibbling at his raw flesh. He could taste the bugs as they crunched between his teeth as he tried to spit them out.

He heard them chewing at his flesh inside his ears. The bugs covered his face, eating through his eyelids. He could see their tiny, sharp jaws as they ate at his eyeballs.

The boy rolled back and forth on the cave floor trying to rid his body of the thousands of insects. As he rolled around, he got closer and closer to the pool of water he had urinated in. Suddenly, he fell over the edge into the cool, clear water.

At first the water stung his raw flesh, but this felt better than the pain of the bites. The insects were washed off him, swimming back to the rocks from where they had come. The boy floated in the safety of the water, wondering if the bugs would attack again.

The water began to heat up and steam started to rise from the surface. The boy tried to swim to the edge, but was overcome by the intense heat. The water started to boil and churned violently, bubbling over the edge and melting the rimstone dam. The smell of cooked flesh filled the cave. All at once the water in the pond started spinning clockwise, forming a whirlpool. Flesh and bones spun round and round, spinning more quickly as it reached the center of the pond. Then it was sucked down into the funnel to the bottom of the pool and onward through cracks, deeper into the earth's core. The water in the pool calmed. The bugs and bats were gone, and so was the young boy.

Off in a distant part of the cave, a small voice could be heard calling for his friend. The second boy sat down to rest. His body was shaking from cold and fear. He thought the worst for his friend after hearing his screams of terror from deep within the cave. Now he feared for himself.

As he sat resting, mud from the cave walls started flying off in large chunks, hitting him and sticking to his body. The mud was very painful as it struck him. No matter where he ran, mud and rock flew from the walls and ceiling. The weight from the mud sticking to his body soon brought him down. He was encased in mud from the neck down. As he lay on the cave floor, he heard a deafening roar.

He stared in disbelief as the ceiling, covered with hundreds of sodastraws, started to slowly lower itself down. Inch by inch, the ceiling came toward his body. He closed his eyes as tightly as he could, hoping he could summon up some unknown power within him to stop the terror that was unfolding. As he opened his eyes and looked up, the first of the long sodastraws pierced his skull. In a matter of seconds, hundreds more pushed through the mud, and into his soft skin and organs.

The cave was silent for a few minutes as the movement stopped. The roar was heard again as the ceiling raised itself back from where it had come. Blood oozed from tiny holes left by the sodastraws. Over the next several hundred years, water would drip onto the boy's body, preserving him in a hard layer of limestone. Explorers years to come would name this formation "The Sleeping Boy."

A cave is a living and breathing place, and must be treated as such. Who knows what unseen forces lie dormant in the strange world of darkness.

19

Digger's Delight

Ronald Cole was a quiet guy, a loner. He would sit in the back at most grotto meetings minding his own business. Most of us didn't pay any attention to him. He was a little weird, but I guess we're all a little weird. All he liked to do was dig and he never went caving with other people. Every once in a while he would bring pictures of his latest discoveries to the meetings and pass them around. Nothing great, just another room or passage he found while digging.

One day Ron was digging in Crossroads Cave. It's one of those small, miserable caves that only beginners like. He had been working on this project for months without any success, digging in a small passage that was blowing a lot of air. One day, without warning, the sides fell in on him. He was able to turn around, but he had to dig his way out. When he got the dirt out of his mouth, he screamed in frustration. He was working so hard, but there didn't seem to be any more passage to find. If only he could make a big discovery. Then people would really look up to him.

He didn't go caving for weeks after that scare. Finally, he got up the nerve to go back in there. On his way into the cave he met an old man.

"Who are you?" Ron asked.

"I'm just a friend, Ron," said the old man.

"How do you know my name?"

"I know everybody's name in these parts."

"Well, what are you doing in here?"

"I'm looking for you, Ron."

"What do you want me for?"

"I believe it is you who wants me, Ron."

"Listen, I don't want you, and I wish you would leave me alone now while I go about my business in this cave."

"I understand you would like to find new passages in here," said the old man.

"How do you know that?"

The old man gave Ron a look that sent a chill down his spine. "I know everything that goes on down here. What is it worth to you to find new passage?"

"What do you mean, what is it worth to me? I have no money to give you, and I own very little of anything of value."

"What about your soul, Ron? Would you trade your soul to find the next Lechuguilla, to be the most popular caver in the world?"

Ron laughed aloud. "Yea, sure old man, you can have my worthless soul, and take this too."

Ron picked up his shovel and hit the stranger over the head, knocking him to the ground. He had tired of the man's games and wanted to get back to his work. The stranger got up and stumbled his way out, leaving a trail of blood on the cave floor.

"Get out of here and don't come back," yelled Ron.

"I'll see you around, Ron," came a low voice from the entrance.

"I go caving to get away from the crazy people, now they're following me into the cave too," thought Ron.

He continued deeper into the cave, and soon forgot all about the crazy old man. He didn't want to dig in the passage that had collapsed. This day he picked a new spot. After about an hour of digging his shovel broke through the back wall. He enlarged the hole enough for him to crawl into the newly found room.

Ron expected just another small, muddy room, just like all the rest he had found. As his light panned across the room he was shocked at what he saw. It was the most beautiful underground room Ron had ever seen. As far as his light could shine, formations of every kind adorned the walls and ceilings. He was too excited to dig anymore that day. He took a whole roll of pictures, and then sealed up the hole leading to the room. Leaving the cave, he saw the trail of blood left by the old man, and laughed to himself.

At the next grotto meeting Ron was a very popular guy. Nobody could believe the beautiful room Ron found in that muddy old cave. For the next several weeks Ron led small groups of cavers to the new room. It was named Ron's Treasure Room from then on.

It seemed Ron had acquired the golden touch. Every week he made more and more discoveries. Every cave he dug in would reveal new passages. It was truly amazing. It was as though he had x-ray vision. It got so that he would have to sneak out at night if he wanted to go caving alone.

He became so popular that he was elected grotto chairman. In the course of a year, Ron had doubled the length of known passage in the state. He even had his picture on the cover of the *NSS News*! It was truly a Cinderella story. The following year he was elected to the Board of Governors of the NSS.

He soon got bored with the caves around home, and moved to New Mexico. Out there he continued to amaze people with his abilities to find new passages. It didn't take long until he connected Lechuguilla Cave to Carlsbad Caverns! This was by far the biggest news to rock the caving scene in a long time. His name and picture became common in every caving circle. By the end of that year he was elected to the position of President of the NSS.

He surprised us all one day by taking a trip back home to visit his old friends. It was like the President of the United States walking into the grotto meeting that night. The meeting stopped and everybody gathered around to hear Ron's stories of caving out west and being the NSS President. They were really proud of Ron. He was a hero.

"I have some unfinished business in Crossroads Cave," said Ron. "I never went back into that passage that collapsed on me. I think that's going to open up into a big cave. It's about time I found out."

Everyone wanted to help Ron dig. He told them he hadn't been caving alone in a long time, and would like to enjoy some quiet time in there.

The following day Ron went into Crossroads Cave. The passage was still there. It looked like nobody had gone into it since the day he dug his way out. He crawled to the end and started digging. Little by little the passage got bigger. Soon he was able to walk. It was a tall fissure passage, trending down. After about a mile of walking, the cave opened up to enormous proportions. Ron was very happy with himself. He knew that cave would open up someday. It just took someone with his luck and skill to make it happen.

"This is what it's all about," thought Ron. "To be where nobody has been, to see what nobody has seen, to be the first. It's like walking on the moon."

Just then he heard a sound come from the shadows of the cave. He turned to see an old man.

"Hello Ron," said the stranger.

"Who are you? Where did you come from?"

"Remember me, Ron? That was a good shot to the head you gave me a few years ago."

Ron was silent for a while. His mind raced to try and remember this old man standing before him in the dim light of the cave.

"You!" yelled Ron. "Why are you following me?"

"I'm here to collect," said the old man.

"Collect what? I've got nothing of yours."

"Oh, but you do have something of mine. We made a deal, remember?"

"I didn't make any deals with you. Now get out of here before I hit you again, and this time you won't get up."

"I don't think that will work this time. You still haven't figured it out have you? It's your soul I want. You traded it to me for all that fame and good luck you've been having. Do you think you found all those new caves and passages by yourself? You were a nobody, a loner. I turned your life around. I gave you that fame, and now I'm here to collect."

Ron lunged at the old man with his shovel. He hit him several times, but the old man just stood there.

"Look around, Ron, and welcome to HELL!" yelled the stranger.

Suddenly, fire exploded up from holes in the floor of the cave. Winged demons swooped down from unseen heights. The deafening screams of millions of trapped souls filled the air. Ron tried to run, but all the passages were gone. He started to dig his way out, but the dirt turned to bones, millions of bones.

The skulls opened their mouths and started to scream. The hands of the dead grabbed at his clothes and pulled him in. He was now surrounded by bones, pulling and ripping his flesh. The skulls were screaming in his ears and chewing at his skin. All he could do was try to dig through the bones.

"Dig, Ron, dig," laughed the voice of the old man.

But for Ron, it was too late. He would be forever trapped in a sea of bone. Forever, digging with the hopes of breaking free of the Devil's hold.

20

Dreamer

The caver laid his head down in bed and closed his eyes, eagerly anticipating the coming night. The dreams had started about one week ago. After several nights, he realized that they were not separate dreams but one continuous dream. Each one started where the last one had left off the night before.

In these dreams he found himself in a wondrous cave. At times he couldn't see the far walls or the ceiling above him. Formations hung from places too high up to see where they started. Flowstone of every color covered the walls and floor. He would walk for miles in these cave dreams, never coming to the end of the cave, just following one long passage that wound on endlessly through the earth. There was no mud or dirt in this cave, just pure limestone hollowed out by tens of thousands of years of water dissolving away the rock.

He never needed a light in the cave, and he never seemed to get tired or hungry. It was just one of those things that only happen in dreams. In the morning, when he awoke, he would feel as refreshed as if he had been on vacation. No matter how bad it got at work, he knew he could escape the real world when he got home and went to sleep. The dream continued for weeks. Every night the cave looked just as beautiful as the last. But this dreaming started to take its toll on the caver.

Where he once woke up refreshed, he now felt more

tired and depressed, wanting just to go back to sleep and not have to deal with the real world. He was fired from his job for sleeping at work.

His body started to look haggard and weak. He would sleep more and eat less. When he woke up, he would take sleeping pills and go back to sleep. In his dreams he felt great with lots of energy. Why deal with the waking world of pain and hunger? This dream world became his real world.

After being missed at a grotto meeting, some old caving friends came by his house one day and found him half dead. They rushed him to the hospital. The doctors there said he had slipped into a coma. They did not know if he would ever wake up. For days he lay in the hospital.

One morning when the doctors came to see him, they found his bed empty. The sheets were all wet and there was a pile of dirt on his pillow. No one knows what became of him. He just disappeared off the face of the earth. So the next time you dream about caving, listen closely. You just might hear his footsteps around the next bend.

21

No Life Here

This report was found aboard a UFO that crashed in a farmer's field, in a small town in West Virginia.

Day 1

I entered a solar system consisting of 9 planets, 44 moons and many asteroids, comets, and other small bodies, all sweeping in regular orbits around a relatively small star.

I have landed on one of the smaller planets. The gravity is very strong, and the atmosphere has a very high oxygen content. Because of these two facts, I do not expect to find intelligent life forms here. I will leave the ship tomorrow and explore this strange new planet.

Day 2

There is much green vegetation here and violent electrical storms. I will prepare to explore further from the ship tomorrow.

Day 3

I have discovered a large life form that walks on two extensions under its large body, and also has two extensions out its sides. It has a small head on top. It lives in crude wooden structures and communicates by use of sound waves. Its method of transportation is a small internal combustion engine, surrounded by a metal frame. It moves slowly on four round rubber disks.

Day 4

I have observed these creatures going into a hole in

the ground. I will get closer and find out where they go.

Day 5,6,7,8

I have watched these creatures for several days now. They all meet at the hole in the ground. They call it a cave. Some climb down the hole and others swing down into it on a rope. They dress in strange clothing and protect their heads with a hard shell before they go into this cave. The hard shell has a light mounted on top of it. They come out looking very dirty and tired. They bring nothing out with them.

Day 9

I followed them into the hole. At the bottom, many trails go horizontally for a long way. It is cold and dark down there. They crawl through mud and water. Some go through very tight places. Sometimes they get stuck. At times they stop and stare at massive walls of calcium carbonate. When they come out, they go to a small wooden structure. They sit around and drink a strange smelling liquid. One of these creatures drank a lot of this liquid and reverted to a very primitive state. This liquid is dangerous.

Day 10

I am preparing to leave. I am done with all testing and have recorded all findings. Life here is at a very early stage of development. I recommend a return trip in about five million years. I have captured one of the cave dwellers. Perhaps with closer study we will find out more about this interesting creature which spends most of its time underground for no apparent reason. I leave with two regrets. They are: there is no intelligent life here and I wish I could have fit through that tight spot to see more of that cave.

22

New Member

I saw him for the first time at our February grotto meeting. He was a small man in his mid fifties. I had joined the club several months ago and didn't know many people at the time. When our eyes met, it sent a chill down my spine. I looked away, but I could still feel the stare of his cold, dark eyes upon me, sizing me up, like a cat slowly stalking it's prey. There was evil in this man. I watched him out of the corner of my eye as he looked over each member in the room. His expression never changed, only very slowly did his eyes and head move from one member to the next. He stared as though he were reading their minds, searching for information locked deep inside.

Suddenly, the chairman stopped talking and dropped to the floor, screaming out in pain. His hands were holding the sides of his head. Blood poured out of his ears, eyes, nose, and mouth. "The stranger was using ESP and melting his brain," I thought!

"Stop it, your killing him," I yelled, as I lunged at the stranger. A friend kicked me and said, "Paul, wake up. The meeting is over."

I woke up on the floor. I had fallen asleep. I looked around the room and saw the chairman laughing with other people. Was it all a dream? There wasn't any blood pouring out of his head. Was the stranger a part of the dream too? He was nowhere to be seen. I had to know.

I asked my friend Jim. "Did you see that strange guy tonight, looking everybody over?"

"Ya, he gave me the creeps."

So it wasn't all a dream. Something told me this guy was going to be trouble. By the time the March meeting rolled around I had forgotten all about him until I walked into the meeting. There he was again, sitting in the same place, in the same chair, looking the same way. I picked a spot where I could watch him, without him seeing me. About halfway through the meeting he finally spoke.

"If anybody is going to Skull Cave, I'd like to go along."

A silence fell upon the group. The words Skull Cave sent a chill through the room, as if the windows and doors had just been opened to the cold winter air outside. Nobody had been to that cave or even said those words in years.

"I don't believe I've meet you before," spoke Bob, our chairman.

"I'm sorry, my name is Jack Landis. I'm from the Death Valley Grotto, and I'm in the area visiting some friends. I thought I would try to do some caving while I'm here."

"Well Jack, it's nice to meet you, but nobody goes in that cave anymore."

"Why not? Is there a problem with the cave?"

"No, no problem with the cave. There was an accident in there several years ago and we, as a grotto, thought it best not to go there anymore."

"Was someone hurt?"

"Yes, one of our members, Don Austin, was killed in there."

"I'm sorry to hear about that, but if that happened years ago, I don't see what harm a trip in there now could do."

"We just don't go there anymore! If you would like to

go there, that's fine with me, but no one in this room will take you!"

The subject of Skull Cave ended, and the stranger got quiet. The meeting wasn't the same after that. It was closed quickly and everyone went home.

I wasn't a member of the grotto at the time of the accident, but I did read about it in the newspapers. The parents were devastated. Don was 16 years old at the time and the only child they could have. After the funeral, his parents hired a big time lawyer who started suing everybody—the town, the grotto, the NSS, the landowner, even the makers of the rope they say broke on him. Then suddenly, all the suits were dropped, and the parents packed up and moved away. That was four years ago, and the last anyone ever talked about Skull Cave until now.

It wasn't a good night for Bob. After everyone had left the meeting at his house, he drank until he passed out on the floor. The dream came back that night too. In the dream he's looking over the edge of the pit, calling to his friend Don who had just fallen to the bottom. He watches as a light slowly floats up from the darkness. Then Don appears in front of him, floating in the air. Blood is pouring from a stalagmite protruding from his head. His outstretched hands are bloody with rope burns that show exposed bone. As he speaks, blood gurgles out his mouth.

"You killed me, Bob. You tied the ropes. You put the harness on me. It's your fault."

Then he grabs Bob by the neck and throws him down into the pit. It's always the same dream, and he always wakes up before he hits the bottom. When he woke up this time, in a drunken haze, his eyes made out a bloody piece of rope lying across his legs. Just then the phone rang. It was his friend, John Wilson.

"Bob, your not going to believe this. When I woke up this morning, on my table was a copy of the newspaper from when Don fell into the pit. And Jim called me and said someone left a message on his answering machine calling him a murderer. I'm getting worried. I think someone knows it wasn't an accident!"

"Shut up, John! It WAS an accident, and don't talk about it on the phone. Go pick up Jim and come over here, we'll talk about it then. I've got an idea."

Within an hour the three cavers were at Bob's house, gathered around his table, with worried looks on their faces.

"For four years we've been able to keep this thing quiet," stated Bob. "None of us have talked, so someone is just messing with us. All this shit happening and that guy showing up at the meeting asking about the cave is more than just a coincidence, if you ask me. We did the right thing back then. Don was going to talk to that reporter about caving, and he would have talked about our new cave. The whole world would have found out about it. It would've gotten trashed. It's the best cave this state has. We all agreed to do it, and we're all in this together. If everyone stays calm we can work this out. Here's my plan. Jim, you announce a trip to Skull Cave in the next meeting notice, and we'll see who goes. Once in the cave, we'll see what happens and do whatever we have to do."

Two weeks later Bob, John, Jim, and I stood by the cave entrance, waiting to see who else would show up for the trip into Skull Cave. I had never been in the cave and jumped at the chance to see it. Just as we were ready to go into the cave, we saw a car coming up the long dirt road. The car stopped several feet in front of us and Jack Landis got out. All of us stared speechless and scared as the stranger from the meeting approached.

"Hi guys. Sorry I'm late. I got a little lost on the way."

"Well, it looks like it's just us," spoke Bob. "We've been waiting here over an hour. Let's get caving."

The five of us followed the path up the mountain to the cave. It was a pit entrance with a 73-foot drop. John rigged the drop while we all put on our gear and checked our equipment. John went down the pit first, followed by Bob and then me. As Jim was ready to drop down, Jack approached him.

"Let me check your knots before you hook in, Jim," asked Jack.

As Jack was going over the knots, in one quick move he slipped a loop of rope over Jim's head, pulled it tight around his neck, and pushed him over the edge of the pit. It was over before Jim could say a word. Jim had fallen about ten feet before the rope went tight and snapped his neck. Jack quickly pulled up the limp body and hid it in the woods. "Two more to go," he mumbled.

When Jack finally reached us at the bottom, he told us Jim was feeling a little light headed, and decided to wait in the car but might catch up with us later if he felt better. After some talk, we started off into the cave. Bob took the lead, followed by me, John, and then Jack. I wanted to keep my distance from the stranger. As usual we would break up at times and explore different parts of the cave. After waiting for close to half an hour for Jack and John to return, Jack finally came back with a note he found stuck on a formation. It read: Feeling sick, didn't want to hold you up. See you on top.— John

Little did we know John was lying somewhere with a 100-pound rock on his head. We decided to go as far as the pit and then turn around—the same pit Don had fallen into. When we reached the pit we all sat down in silence. Even the stranger was silent. Bob looked very nervous. Suddenly, Jack bumped into Bob, sending him sliding down the slope towards the pit. Jack quickly grabbed the back of Bob's collar, holding him suspended over the pit.

"Well Bob," the stranger said coldly and calmly. "Isn't

this funny."

"Please pull me up," pleaded Bob.

"Tell me Bob, what did happen to Don that day?"

"Please pull me up, I'll tell you all you want to know."

"Did you cut the rope or just tie some bad knots?"

"I don't know what you're talking about. Now pull me up."

Bob looked to me. "Paul, tell him to pull me up, please help me!"

Before I could say a word, Jack let go of Bob. Bob's screams echoed from the pit, until he hit bottom. It was just me and Jack now. He turned to me and said, "I will not hurt you. You were not one of them. The other two are dead also. You'll find them if you look hard enough."

The only word I could get out of my mouth was, "Why?"

Slowly, before my eyes, the old man turned into the form of Don Austin. It was the face I remembered from the newspaper articles years ago.

"They killed me and afterwards my parents died from a broken heart. It was a simple matter of revenge."

"What am I suppose to do now? Everyone will think I did this."

"Tell them you saw Jack Landis do it."

With that said, he stood up, walked right through the wall, and disappeared.

23

If Stephen King went caving

I entered the cave at midnight with Paul Steward and John Tudek as my trusted guides. Large, brown, flea-bitten rats were seen in the light of a full moon, scurrying about the entrance with bits of blood-soaked meat hanging from their mouths, chewed off from a fresh roadkill. Vampire bats circled in the sky with rabies infested saliva dripping from their sharp, white teeth. With each beat of their wings, clouds of lice fell from their small, hairy bodies.

The cave walls were cool to the touch, like the hardened skin of a cadaver lying in a dark morgue. The air was damp with a musty, pungent odor, like that of a dungeon with earthen walls. The passage floor was covered with a deep, sticky mud, having the consistency of coagulated blood. But the most menacing presence was the darkness. A dark so thick and heavy you could cut it with a sharp knife. When God said, "let there be light," he had reasons for not allowing it down here. We were in the Devil's territory. I could feel him close to us, lurking in the dark recesses of the cave, waiting for the right moment to suck out our souls. This was his land, and we would have to abide by his rules—for now. In the high, vaulted ceilings of the cave our voices echoed, like the cries of prisoners dying in a madman's torture chamber. This was a horrid place where man should not trespass. The underground is for the dead and buried, not the living.

Deeper into this tomb of dirt, our journey continued with feelings of impending danger around every corner. Our lights cast ominous shadows that danced on the passage walls. Only darkness marked our way through these catacombs of hell. The air was electrified by an evil force, pulling us deep into the bowels of the earth. I soon realized we were lost in a maddening maze of twisting, turning passages and returning back to the surface might not be an option for our group.

In the inky blackness, our lights exposed yellow, sinister eyes gazing down upon us, following our every move. We could hear the sound of their long, curled nails, scraping the rocks as they climbed down from their unseen roosts. These hideous freaks of nature, part man part beast, concealed from the outside world, feasted on the bodies of lost cavers once their souls were taken. They would not attack yet.

The passage narrowed to a low crawlway. The razor-sharp edges of the scalloped walls cut through my clothes, scraping the skin from my bones. The oozing blood cooled quickly, chilling my overheated body. Death was near, I could smell it in the air. One feels most alive when death is close at hand; I turned to find I was alone. Alone in this godforsaken world of eternal darkness. Panic gripped me. My chest felt heavy as I tried to breathe. My dark world started spinning out of control. I was caught in the hands of fear. Then, from the shadows came a lone, icy voice that spoke out to me.

"Good evening, Mr. King, and welcome. It's such a pleasant surprise."

In the haze of my light stood the supreme ruler of the underground. The Sultan of Sin, The Dealer of Death. The Honorable Mister D. himself. He looked like a rather meek old man except for his eyes. I could see the bright fires of hell raging in his pupils.

"I've read all your books, Stephen. I feel like we know each other. You've made me out to be such a horrible person. I'm really a nice guy, once you get to know me. I do hope you'll stay for awhile."

With that said, he grabbed my head with both his hands. A wave of hot pain seared through every inch of my body. His fingers were like leeches, sucking out all the good memories of my lifetime, leaving me with only bad memories and pain. All the cuts and bruises I ever had returned, oozing burning blood. As his hands let go of me it felt like I was being sucked into a bottomless black hole, condemned into hell.

Suddenly, two lights appeared from out of the dark. It was Paul and John. They were alive! I was saved! "I'm over here, guys," I yelled. They looked at me strangely.

"Get a grip on yourself, Stephen, this is only the entrance tube," spoke Paul.

"What a wuss," John whispered.

24

Dark Greed

This story was co-written with John Tudek, over several months of e-mail.

Light from the full moon rising above their heads illuminated the group of cavers as they approached the cave entrance. Long, eerie, grotesque shadows were cast on the quarry wall. Their warm breath formed a fog that swirled around their heads as they walked along in single file. The silence of the cold winter night was shattered by a flock of sleeping vultures, awakened by the crunch of leaves from under foot. The beating of their wings echoed off the tree tops as the large birds took to flight.

Vultures, winged messengers of death. The sight of this bird is synonymous with death, not the causing of death, but the following of it. Their life depends upon their ability to seek out the dead and dying, to sense its presence and to feed off it. The birds circled several times overhead and then disappeared into the night sky. Their cries echoed in the distance off the surrounding hills.

Was this an omen for what was yet to come? Paul thought.

Paul and John gathered together the group of new cavers and led them into the warmth of the cave. It was a walk-in entrance, about four feet high and three feet wide. Just inside, it opened up to about ten feet high. There were seven in the group. A lucky number, John thought. They turned on their lights as they went in. There was some oohing and aahing as John fired up his carbide lamp. As far as he could tell, he was the only carbide caver in the group. The bright, starry sky was replaced by a dull, gray roof.

Once inside, one of the newcomers shrieked. John looked back and saw she was pointing at the ceiling. Seven feet above where she stood was a hole leading up to a higher level of the cave. Lots of people had tried to get into this hole, but as it was away from all walls, it could only be climbed into with a ladder. Besides, it had been surveyed and went nowhere. John looked up into the hole. At its edge was a large, leather-winged bat. John chuckled. "It's just a bat."

"No," she whispered. "I saw eyes."

"It's probably just your light reflecting off the wet flowstone," Paul said. "The walls play tricks on your eyes sometimes."

Paul looked towards the passage they were to head into and saw a puddle was cloudy. "Someone had been through here lately," he thought.

"Cmon guys," John called out. He was in the lead now, a few feet in front of the rest. "This cave isn't going to explore itself. With any luck, we'll make the Pirate Room in under 40 minutes."

"The Pirate Room?" a newcomer inquired.

"Yep, the Pirate Room. All sorts of scary things have happened in this cave. Some say it is haunted by a pirate named Silverpatch. Locals say he left his gold buried somewhere in this cave. Of course, that's silly. We're a good 40 or 50 miles from the coast, and . . . well, Paul likes scary stories. You tell it Paul, tell about old Silverpatch's untimely subterranean demise."

"Well, according to local legends, Silverpatch and his band of pirates were anchored off the coast. His men accused Silverpatch of cheating on dividing up the gold they had just stolen. After several days of drinking, the men decided to have a mutiny. So, they took over the ship and tied up Silverpatch. They were going to hang him the next day, but he got away that night and headed to shore in a small boat with the gold. When they found out he was gone they set out to find him. It wasn't hard following his trail of rape, murder, robbery, and spending of the gold. The trail finally ended in this town. When they found him, he ran off and headed to this cave. Now comes the good part. They say his men chased him into here, but Silverpatch, the gold, and his men were never seen again. Some say the ghosts of him and his men are still in here guarding the gold. Every once in awhile someone says they see or hear a ghost in the Pirate Room."

You could hear a pin drop as Paul was telling his story. The group stared wide-eyed, hanging on his every word.

"I really don't think Silverpatch could have carried all his gold this far from the coast. I've been all through this cave, and never found any sign of treasure."

"Have you ever seen a ghost in here?" one from the group asked.

"Let's just say, I don't believe in ghosts. Now let's get going. I'm starting to get cold sitting here," Paul said. "Lead the way, John; I'll bring up the rear."

The group traveled through several large rooms and a few tight crawlways. They were doing quite well for new cavers. Suddenly, John's foot stumbled over a loose rock and he fell face down. He found himself staring at a hole in the floor, barely large enough for a man to fit into. The hole was filled with bats. John backed away from the little hole and a pebble fell down it. The bats awoke and began screeching. Their deafening sounds echoing in the passage. As the party stared, a column of the winged rodents rose from the hole and headed directly at them.

The new cavers screamed, and the girls cowered low to the ground. John simply sat there as the bats flew around him, close enough that the tips of their wings touched his hair. In a few moments the terror subsided and all was quiet again. Yet all was not well. The new cavers had been thoroughly frightened and were talking about going back. John ignored them all, and crept back to the edge of the hole. It seemed bigger now that the bats were gone, and he could see a large passage at the bottom. There were also some boards on the floor of the lower level. John noticed there were recent digging and scraping marks on the walls of the hole.

"Hey Paul," John whispered with awe. "Come and look at this."

"Well, what do you know," Paul said. "I must have walked over that hole a hundred times and never looked down it. Looks like you just found another passage in this old cave. Since you found it, you can have the honors of being the first to check it out."

"I think we've had enough of this cave today," said one from the group.

One by one, all the group agreed they were ready to leave. The stories of pirates, ghosts, gold, and now the bats, was all the group could take for this trip.

"I tell you what," Paul said. "Everybody sit tight. Give us ten minutes to check out this hole. Then we'll have you out in no time. Take out your food and have a bite to eat. This won't take us long."

John took out his webbing, tied one end to a rock, and let the other end drop down into the hole. He wrapped the webbing around himself and did a body rappel down into the blackness. After several minutes his light appeared from below.

"Paul, you're not going to believe this! I found a large room down here with a lake. A deep stream leads off from the lake into darkness. The best part is there's a boat tied up to a rock!"

"Yaaaa . . ., sure John. Is there any gold, and a few dead pirates down there too?" Paul asked.

Just then an explosion was heard coming from the direction of the entrance.

"WHAT the hell was that?" John screamed from the pit. "Sounds like the whole damn cave blew up!"

Above, there was panic. The new cavers shouted and screamed as Paul tried to calm them down. He gave one girl a slap when she refused to stop wailing, and violently shook one of the guys until he returned to normal.

"Listen to me! Listen to me!" Paul shouted, trying to get order into the group. He knew that without order all these new cavers would never see daylight again, and he probably wouldn't either. His mind slipped into rescue mode, and he began to take on the persona of a wilderness survival guy, almost identical to any of the personalities he'd read about. After what seemed an eternity, John climbed out of the pit. He found the party sitting quietly with Paul watching over them like a guard dog. They were either too afraid or too awed to do anything but obey.

"Everything okay?" John asked.

Paul nodded with a worried look.

"Um, Paul, I have a stupid question. What happened to the breeze?"

Paul felt the air a moment. John was right. There was no breeze. There is always a breeze in the main passage. It leads into an impassable crack, just like in Jewel Cave. But the breeze was gone, cut off abruptly.

"The only way that could have happened was if the whole side of the mountain collapsed," said John.

"I lied about what's down there, too. There's no lake or boat. It's a small dome room with a stream coming in one side and out the other. The insurgence is a crack. The resurgence is a low cobble crawl. You'd get the ribs wet.

And, Paul . . . I never thought I'd say this about a cave trip. We're screwed."

"We're not screwed yet," Paul replied. "Everybody is alive, and no one is hurt. We just have to stay warm. Everyone take out all your food. Let's see what we have."

As usual the new cavers brought more food then they would need, lots of sandwiches and candy bars. Paul picked the thinnest caver to collect the food and watch over it, for obvious reasons.

"Starting now, said Paul, we ration the food and eat only once a day. We don't know how long we're going to be in here. Water won't be a problem, there's lots down below, according to John."

Paul looked down the passage leading to the entrance. A cloud of dust hung in the air from the explosion. Paul and John walked away from the group to talk.

"John, I want to go down and check out that stream passage you saw. I'm a little smaller than you, maybe I could push it. I think you should go check out the entrance. Maybe it's not as bad as we think. Splitting up isn't good, but time is our enemy now. We have to find out where we stand, as fast as we can. These kids are going to start freaking on us soon."

"How long do you really think we can survive in here?" John asked.

"I don't know, three, four days? It depends on how tough this group is."

"Where's Sherri?" asked one from the group.

"What do you mean, where's Sherri?" Paul replied.

"She's gone. She was here a minute ago and now she's gone."

"GREAT! Now we've got someone lost, too! If you guys want to live then I suggest everybody stay right where you are. DO NOT MOVE FROM THIS ROOM! John, you better get going, maybe you'll find her on the way. She

97

can't be too far. Be careful, there may be a lot of unstable places in here now, and we may have company in here, too."

"Now listen up, everybody," Paul continued. "I'm going down that hole to look for another way out of here. Everybody sit close to each other for warmth, don't leave, don't eat any of our food, and a prayer or two wouldn't hurt."

"Paul, do you believe in heaven?" asked one new caver.

"I'm not sure about heaven, but I'm starting to believe in hell." Paul replied.

Paul disappeared down the hole. "Already they're thinking about dying. I hope John has luck," Paul thought.

"I don't think leaving you guys alone is a good idea now," John spoke. "Everybody get up, you're coming with me. You'll stay warmer if we move around."

John wasn't actively considering dying just yet, but it was in the back of his head. He gathered up the party and began the trip back up to the entrance. The march was like a funeral procession, silent, with heads hanging low. It was not a long trip, and the procession seemed to travel outside of time. Eventually, they reached areas that even the newcomers recognized, and they slowed down. Ahead of them the room was filled with smoke and haze; small rocks littered the floor.

"Come on," John grunted. "Let's see if we can dig ourselves out."

As they reached the breakdown pile, John suspected that it should have been smokier. He smelled gunpowder, but it seemed distant.

"Maybe it's nct that bad," he thought. "Everybody look around. Look for places where the smoke is moving."

John looked up at the hole in the roof, where that girl

had seen the eyes before. The smoke seemed to be swirling up there. "Maybe there is more to that hole," John thought.

Back in the lower level, Paul was making progress. He built a small dam on the far side of the dome room to stop the flow of water. The loose cobble was easily scooped aside, as he belly crawled in the ten-inch-high passage. As far as his light could see, the passage continued on. Backing up would be next to impossible without help. Several hundred feet into the passage the cobble started to mix with a loose sand. Farther on the cobble was replaced with a moist sandy floor. He could feel a light breeze on his face as he crawled. Digging in the sandy passage, his hand grabbed at something hard. He let the sand sift through his fingers as he adjusted his light to his hand. There in his open hand was a small gold coin.

In the dome room, the dam was being smashed apart. Backed up waters rushed across the room, filling the low passage to the ceiling.

"This should fix that one," a voice whispered. "Now to the others."

John's group placed rocks in the center of the room. He hoped they could stack them high enough to reach the hole in the ceiling. A trick he learned from Floyd Collins. After fifteen minutes the pile was four feet high, and most of the group was suffering from smoke inhalation. John found that he could grab a protrusion with his hand from the very top of the pile, and pull himself up part way. He got one of the bigger people to give him a boost and he was up into the hole.

"Stay here. This will only take a minute," said John.

John had a theory. He hoped that the rockslide occurred right above the entrance. If it did, then the crawlway he was in might now lead to the outside world. He recalled the very end of the crawlway being a small room, warmer than the rest of the cave, with many roots in the wall. It had a dirt ceiling, and the survey put it less than five feet from the surface. John noticed the air was cleaner as he got up into the tube, and felt a slight breeze where before he knew there to be none. He reached the end of the crawlway, and an idea struck him. He extinguished his carbide lamp, and let his eyes adjust to the darkness. Now he could see vague shadows, and cracks of light coming from the far wall. He found the biggest and re-lit his lamp. It was coming from a place where the wall had slumped and the roots were in chaos. He pulled a shovel from his pack and began digging. It was scary work. The more he dug, the more dirt fell on him. However, he felt a definite breeze moving through the dirt and after several minutes of digging, a crack of moonlight invaded the room. John crawled back to the hole, and called for the others to come up. As they arrived, John sent them to dig. Less than an hour after they had left Paul, they were outside.

"What does it look like?" John asked from inside. He was cleaning up his shovel and collecting his things.

"It's a mess," one of them answered. "It looks like most of the hill came down. The tree that was right here got uprooted, that's why it was so easy to get out."

"OK, listen to me good. Go into town immediately, get the sheriff, and give him this number."

John passed out the eastern cave rescue call out number.

"We still have two people in the cave, and this is a rescue situation. I'm going to find Paul and Sherri, and get them out. Do this, okay?"

They all nodded. John took one longing look at the moon, grimaced, and disappeared back into the cave. He wondered if he would see it again. He made sure the rope was tight, and slid back down into the room. He looked at his watch. Paul had been left alone for over an hour. John hoped he was OK. Without looking back, he ran down the passage.

Behind him, a hand reached down from above. Slowly, it pulled the rope, length by length, up into the hole, until it was all gone. It was a woman's hand, with red fingernails. A voice whispered down from the hole. "Now go and finish him. I'll take care of the rest."

Paul first sensed something was wrong when his legs started getting wet. Quickly, the water was several inches deep and rising. He crawled like a madman as the passage filled. He was forced to turn over on his back, and crawl with his nose as close to the ceiling as possible, scrapping it raw against the jagged rocks. The surging water continued to rise, he could go no farther. He found a crack in the ceiling and jammed his nose up into it. The water completely filled the passage. For several minutes he held onto rocks, breathing shallow breaths from inside the crack. Slowly, the water started to recede and soon it was only an inch deep. He crawled on in the wet passage until he heard something ahead. He lay still waiting to hear the noise again. Looking around he realized he was in a large room. The noise he had heard was his own echo. It felt good to stand as he explored the room. He was amazed his hand still held the gold coin he had found. It was a Spanish doubloon. Could the gold stories really be true? Paul thought. His eyes caught sight of something white across the room. He walked over and picked it up. It was a human skull.

John made it back to the room where he had left Paul, who was nowhere to be seen. John called for a few minutes, but there was no answer. The room was deserted and he wasn't able to make out the freshest set of tracks. Quickly he dropped down into the hole. At the bottom, he found the stream, and noticed the broken dam. He pushed his head down the stream passage and called for his friend. The stream however was too noisy. John stared down the passage, looking for some clue that Paul had passed this way. He didn't want to try it unless he knew Paul was down there, otherwise he'd get soaked for no reason at all. He spent many minutes looking down the crawlway, until his straining eyes caught sight of something shiny. Thinking it could be a mini-mag, he sucked in his stomach, and began the wet crawl down the passage. It wasn't a mini-mag, but it was equally impressive. A shiny gold coin, cleaned from the stream. Farther ahead, he saw dirt pushed aside, and scuff marks on the roof. "Maybe Paul did come this way," he thought. He redoubled his efforts through the hole, and pushed his way through the water and cobble. When he finally popped into the big room, his body was soaked. He stumbled to his feet, and spit out a mouthful of stream.

"PAUL!" he called out at the top of his lungs. No answer. John looked at his feet. A skull poked out of the sand. John bent over to pick it up. There were tracks leading away from it. Tracks could only mean one person. John dropped the skull and ran off, shouting as he went.

Shouts of joy were heard from the group as Sherri popped out of the hole they had dug. She was hit with questions from the group. "Where have you been? What happened to you? Are you OK?"

They told her of all that had happened, the explosion, the digging, and John going back into the cave to look for Paul and her.

"We were just on our way to go call the police and give them this number John gave us."

"I feel so bad getting lost from you guys. Can I help out and go call the police for you? It's the least I can do."

Nobody really wanted to leave and go find a phone, so

she was given the job. A smile was forming on her face as she headed off out of the quarry with the one phone number that could save someone's life.

"Now Bill will have time to finish off those two in the cave," she whispered.

The rest of the group huddled together in the chilly air, waiting for Paul and John to appear from the cave. The vultures had returned and were seen in the moonlight, circling overhead.

Paul stopped in his tracks and listened. He thought he heard a sound coming from behind him. There was another thump and Paul now knew there was someone coming. He was all set to greet this person, when his mind began reminding him of a few facts. There was an explosion. Sherri was missing. Somebody had dug open the pit, and someone's skull was lying back there in the passage. The whole cave began to feel sinister, and Paul began to think better of waiting out in the open for this new caver. He looked about and found a small alcove. Cautiously, quietly, he turned off his light, and hid in the gloom. A moment later, a bright electric light filled the passage around the bend. A figure—tall, quick and muscular; clad in cave clothes; and wearing a helmet—ran around the corner into view. Paul watched him glance nervously around, and then scramble up into a small hole in the ceiling. As the stranger was climbing, Paul noticed a gun in the man's belt. The stranger hid himself in the shaft, where he commanded a fairly good view of the passage after the bend. He removed the gun and checked it, felt satisfied, and turned off his light.

Back down the passage another series of noises was coming and coming quickly. There was also a dull glow from that direction, and Paul knew it was the light of a carbide lamp. Someone was setting a trap. And the trap was likely to get them killed. "It must be John coming," he hoped. Quickly, he took the gold coin he found and threw it in the dark towards the bend in the passage. It landed with a light slap, sounding more like a drip of water from the ceiling. Paul hoped John would see the coin and stop to pick it up, giving him a few more seconds to finish his plan. Paul quietly reached down, grabbed a handful of mud, and formed two large mud balls. As planned, John saw the shiny gold coin and stopped to pick it up. This gave Paul time to get into position. Paul thought back to his days as pitcher for the high school baseball team. "Don't fail me now, arm. It's the ninth inning, bases loaded, miss this one and you die."

Paul's arm was cocked and ready. Just as John's light appeared around the bend, the mud ball was in the air. It hit its mark, smothering out John's light and putting the room in complete darkness. The force of the mud ball knocked John's head back, sending him to the floor. A shot rang out, and a streak of light flashed across the room. John yelled, as the bullet ricocheted off his helmet. The helmet shattered, sending pieces of fiberglass into his scalp. As the gun went off, it gave Paul his next target. He threw his last mud ball up into the small hole. There was a yell and a thud as the man lost his grip and fell to the cave floor. Except for a ringing in his ear, the cave was silent and dark. Nobody moved. Paul's mind raced. Was John dead? Was the stranger dead or hurt? Was a gun aimed, ready to shoot at the first sound?

A wave of pain seared through John's scalp, and he fell to the floor in a heap. His helmet lay broken and discarded, his head bare and bleeding. The helmet deflected some of the blow, and the bullet only grazed his skull. He rolled around on the mud floor, screaming without sound for what seemed an eternity. He rolled against a rock and over his pack. Some of his senses returned and he heard a second thwack of mud and something fall with a thud and a groan. John wasn't thinking straight, but he was painfully aware he'd been shot. Instincts, generations suppressed, rose up again, and a combination of anger, revenge, and fear welled up within him. Without any clear sense of direction, he fumbled for his pack. Leaning against the rock for protection, he began to quietly pull things out of his pack. He recognized every container by its shape, heft, and odor. He pulled out that which he needed, and set to work.

Paul remained in his perch, unsure of what to do next. Everyone was doing his best to keep quiet. Paul leaned forward to listen better. There were two distinct sounds coming from the main passage. Back towards John, he heard the rustling of someone's pack. He hoped that his friend was looking for a place to hide. In the other direction however, he heard the sounds of a body slowly rising, of bullets being loaded into a chamber, and footsteps walking towards the pack sounds. Paul settled back for a moment and began to collect a little more mud. Maybe it could work again, he thought.

John heard the footsteps cautiously and quietly moving towards him. His hands were trembling as he prepared his surprise, but more than that, there was another feeling. The hunter instinct was showing itself. Laid across his legs were his two presents, prepared. He reached into his pack for one last surprise and pulled out his geologist's pick. He drove the pick though his belt loop, and picked up the smaller present. He ducked low behind the rock and withdrew his lighter. A glow as blinding as day erupted in the pitch blackness for a moment as John lit the candy wrapper fuse attached to the zip-loc bag. The stranger caught the glow in the corner of his eye and watched it arc across the room, and land in the mud bank on the far side. Paul saw it too, and saw the bag explode a second later in an incendiary blast. The stranger shielded his eyes a moment from the light, his attention turned away from the rock. There was a guttural scream, and John flung himself over the rock, a second flaming zip-loc bag in his hand. The stranger shrieked in fear, and backpedaled, firing his gun wildly. Paul was mesmerized by his friend. There was a long gash down his scalp, and blood caked to his one cheek. He had a ferocious, animalistic, savage look and he came on like a rabid wolf. One of the shots hit John, catching him in the right shoulder. The bag was flung forward, toward the stranger. He tried to avoid it, but his footing gave way in the soft mud and he stumbled. The bag hurtled though the air like a comet aimed at the stranger's face, exploding directly in front of him. There was a deafening explosion, and the room was suddenly flooded once again with a bright light. The strangers face and head were incinerated, a blackened scalp hit the ground a moment later. Paul turned away from the explosion, and then surveyed the scene again. There was some light from the stranger's burning hair, and Paul felt the incredible need for an electric light to be on. He twisted his lamp on, and went to look for John.

He found John on his back, face burned by the explosion. The look was gone, save for a twisted grin that spoke volumes. Paul would have trouble thinking of his friend the same way again. Now however, he was more concerned with simply getting him to safety. John coughed and blood came up. "Spare car . . . bide in pack. Heeaat."

"Just lie still, John. We're going to fix you up. First I need to borrow your pick for a minute."

The man on the cave floor moaned softly. The gun was still in his hand with a finger against the trigger. Paul stood over the man, and looked down. Without any remorse he raised his arm and plunged the pick deep into the strangers skull, killing him instantly. "You picked the wrong cave to go into today, buddy."

Paul turned his attention back to John. He got his lamp cleaned and working, and was trying to get him warm.

"Is he dead, Paul?"

"Ya, I just had to pick his brain a little. I don't think you want your pick back, sorry."

"That was a nice carbide bomb you made."

"Thanks, I didn't know you could throw mud that well."

"I always was good at mud slinging."

"We gotta work on getting you out of here, you look like hell. It looks like you took a bullet in the shoulder, too. Try to stand, and see how it feels."

"Help me up." John instructed.

Paul slid under John's good shoulder and helped him to his feet. John giggled.

"What?" Paul grinned.

"I just saw, pick his brain, pretty good." John stumbled over to the corpse, and removed the pick. He wiped it on the corpse's pants. "It's too good a pick to waste on him. Now let's move the body over, under that breakdown. It seems we get to test your theory about hiding the dead underground."

The two began dragging the corpse. Paul did most of the work. John helped as much as he could with one good arm. "I never thought I'd be living one of my stories," Paul mumbled.

As Paul was picking up rocks and piling them on the body, he spotted more gold coins in the breakdown.

"John, look at this. There're gold coins all over the floor in this room. How much do you think we can get for these?"

"Nothing, if we don't get out of here. We can come back later. Let's get out of here while I still have some strength left in me. I don't want to crawl back down that wet passage with this arm. Let's see where the rest of this cave goes."

Paul shoved the coins deep into his pocket. The two headed off across the room and down the largest of the side passages. The trail was marked by blood dripping from John's arm.

"Hey Paul," John began as they paused for a moment. "I never told you about what I found at the entrance."

"Yeah, where is everyone else?"

"They got out already. But from what I could tell, the whole side of the hill slid down over the entrance."

"What? How? Hills don't do that!"

"I know, and I was thinking, if the entrance back there is sealed, and I bet that guy we killed helped seal it, he wouldn't have sealed himself in the cave. Then there . . ."

"Must be a second entrance," Paul finished.

"Exactly. And, Paul, he may have some friends in here too."

Paul nodded and they continued on. Around the next bend they came to a room with a series of domes in the roof. From one dome, a rope dangled, vertical gear was scattered around the floor.

"Have you ever used a rope walker system to climb up a rope, John?"

"No, and how am I going to climb with this arm?"

"With this system you don't use your arms, just your legs. Let's look through these packs. There must be ascending gear in them."

They found all the gear they needed to climb up the rope. After putting on the gear, John went up first. It looked like about a 40-foot climb. Paul followed behind John with the packs hanging from his harness. Blood dripped on Paul's face from John's wound.

"I'm not going to let you die in here, John," Paul thought. "These people are going to have a big surprise when they come back and find their gear gone."

After Paul was over the top he pulled the rope up, leaving anyone below trapped. From the top of the dome they could smell and feel the cool night air. It didn't take long until they found the entrance. Just as Paul was sticking his head through the entrance a gun was shoved in his face. Long red finger nails wrapped around the trigger. "Going somewhere, boys?" a female voice asked.

Paul looked her in the eye. "You can only kill one of us Sherri, assuming you kill with the first shot. The other one will have you disarmed before you get off another round. Give up now, and you're likely to get off with only a few years. Pull that trigger and someday soon someone will be hooking you up to a million volts of electrified death."

"You're bluffing," she sneered. "You wouldn't risk it!"

"Wouldn't we? Look at us! Look at our bodies! Look at John's arm! Do you think we fear the end for even a moment? We've been grappling with the Reaper since we entered this cave, and he hasn't caught us yet! You're good, lady, but not that good!"

But Sherri was no longer paying attention to Paul. Instead, a twisted smile came over her. Paul paused for a moment, wondering why she was so pleased with herself at this particular moment. John figured it out first.

"Duck," John shouted, and Paul hit the ground. A bullet passed over his head from behind, and narrowly missed Sherri. John already had his pick out, and was upon the assailant. He was a big man, but John's rock hammer proved to be an equalizer. With the first swing, he hit the man's hand, disarming him. Paul was about to join in the fray when he saw Sherri trying to leave from the corner of his eye.

Paul turned and ran down the ridge after her. He saw her ahead, scrambling down the hill in the moonlight. In the distance he could hear the sounds of John's struggle fading fast. As he neared Sherri, he heard two gunshots ring out with finality from behind. Paul hoped for a minute that everything had turned out okay for John. With one final leap, Paul tackled Sherri, and they rolled together down the hill. When they came to rest, Paul grabbed her head and slammed it against the rocky ground. He heard bone crack and splinter as her head snapped back. She was out cold. He blond hair turned crimson red. Paul grabbed her arm and started dragging her back to the cave.

At the cave, the man found the gun Sherri had dropped, and fired two shots at John's feet. John froze with both hands up in the air. "Back in the cave there, Bat Boy, and don't try anything funny or I'll increase your weight by a few ounces."

The man led John through the cave to the edge of the pit. Following directions, John threw the rope back into the pit, and rapelled down with the man following.

"Now what?" John asked.

"Shut up and get moving, kid. I know another way out of here. We'll be long gone by the time anyone tries to find us."

"Fine. Oh, by the way," said John. "See that pile of rocks over there? If you look closely you can see a hand sticking out. I think that's a friend of yours. He had a problem with a rock pick in his skull, but I took it out for him. He twitched a little when I removed it. I'll bet it really hurt."

The man froze as rage built up inside of him. It was the one split second John was waiting for. With his good arm he pushed the man against the wall, and quickly picked up a rock. Three shots rang out as the man went down. The rock John had thrown hit its mark on the man's skull. The bullets missed John and ricochet around the room, splitting one of the breakdown blocks. John walked over and kicked the block. Two sides of the large block broke away, revealing a chest. There was the lost treasure, hidden in a mud ball, and encased in a limestone shell from water dripping on it for years and years.

John heard a few small stones falling into the pit. He picked up the man's gun and hid in the shadows. Someone was coming down the rope. He watched the rope quiver in the gloom, and aimed the pistol. The cone of an electric light came into view, and he got into position, ready to pull the trigger.

"BANG!" John shouted, as Paul whipped around and launched another mud ball that caught John dead between the eyes. John burst out laughing, and dropped the gun. "Ya got me, sheriff," he tried to say between the laughs. Paul couldn't help but laugh, too. After everything, it felt almost necessary to have a release, to laugh. John pointed the chest out to Paul.

"So now what?" John asked. "I mean, I know we did right, but it's going to take forever to prove, and people will never look at us the same anyway. Like it or not, this day has forever changed our lives."

"I know," Paul replied. "It makes me wish it never happened." Paul looked to the chest and back to John . . . "Not."

John grinned. "It wouldn't be that hard, you know."

Epilogue:
    It was a warm autumn day, many, many years later. The small group was dressed mostly in black, and gathered around an open grave. The coffin was made from fine wood, and the handles were cast from real gold. As the coffin was laid to rest, dirt was tossed onto it, slowly filling the hole.

    "And so we return to that from which we came," intoned the Reverend. "Especially true in this case."

    The grave was filled and the group began to slowly

part. As they broke, two smartly dressed figures could be seen on the far side, standing slightly away from the rest of the mourners. One was a young man with brown hair, athletic, thin, perhaps seventeen at most. The other was a thin, ancient figure. White hair now stood where once blonde lay. A short beard covered the base of his chin, and he walked with a stoop. One of his shoulders did not move quite right. They had been quietly talking through most of the ceremony and some of the others may have disapproved. But the deceased would have been happy. They were talking about caves.

"And then what happened?" the young man asked.

"Well, Paul, when we returned to the entrance, we found the girl had died from her wounds. So, we dragged her into the cave and hid her, too. Then we blasted the cave shut. It was not that hard. The entrances were unstable already. Yes, we had to answer a lot of questions afterwards, but the investigation never got very far. We waited a long time, years in fact."

"Waited for what? The cave was blasted shut."

John grinned. "But then, where was that last guy taking me? Didn't he mention something about another entrance as he dragged me through the cave? Paul, it took us years to find it, and when we finally did, we were as surprised as could be. But we weren't just caving for kicks. We knew that somewhere deep in that mountain was Silverpatch's treasure. We wanted to be rich."

"But dad said grandpa made his money off his books."

"Oh, your grandfather made a lot of money from writing, later on. But early, it was the treasure. Your grandparents, however, didn't feel comfortable telling Brian such a gruesome story so early in his life, so they waited. When he was old enough to be told the true story, he didn't believe it. Of course by that time he wasn't interested in caving that much, and Paul was looking more towards his namesake to carry on the story."

Paul blushed as he thought of his grandfather, whom he had idolized as long as he could remember. He found it incredible that a Steward could live and not love caving. John watched him reminisce quietly about his old friend. "Of course, you're everything he could have hoped for."

Paul thought about this, trying to let it sink in. It was all so much. It was like trying to absorb the maps of Mammoth, Jewel, and Lechuguilla Caves all at once. It made his head spin. "And it's all really true?" he found himself asking.

John nodded, and reached into his pocket. Pulling it out, he offered it to Paul. Paul picked it up by the chain. It was delicate and golden, and from the end spun a round, gold disc. Carved into the disk was a picture of the King of Spain. The year on the coin was 1521.

"Wow." Paul mouthed.

"It's yours to keep. It's the coin that your grandfather tossed onto the ground in front of me, so I wouldn't get shot. I kept it, framed it, and gave it to him as a gift. He wanted me to give it to you."

Paul put it on over his head, and tucked it into his shirt.

"Now, I do believe you have a plane to catch young friend. After all, this month's cave trip won't wait up for you. Now, tell me again about this stream passage you were exploring . . . "

25

Hell Tour

Fifteen people walked impatiently up and down the isles of the gift shop, checking their watches and throwing disgusted looks towards the cashier. After a 35-minute delay the overhead intercom finally crackled to life.

"All those for the 11 o'clock tour, please assemble near the steps in the rear of the store."

A small, middle aged woman quickly lead the group down the steps, where she gathered them together in a small waiting room.

"I'd like to welcome everyone to Gory Caverns. My name is Mary, and I'll be your guide today. I do apologize for the delay. I'm sorry to say an elderly lady had a heart attack and died on our last tour. So, I will repeat what you have all been told. If you are pregnant; have a heart condition; or feel uncomfortable in the dark, around bats, or in confined spaces, then I don't recommend this tour for you. You may leave now, and get a full refund of your money. I will tell you, no one has ever died on one of my tours, yet."

She laughed to herself and turned to unlock the big, rusty steel door. It opened with a crusty, squeaking sound, sending chills through the group. Once they were inside, she slammed the door tight and locked it. With her flashlight on, she found the circuit breakers and turned on the lights. A string of bare light bulbs hung from the ceiling, stretching out as far as one could see, illuminating the passage ahead of them. Many of the bulbs were blown out, while some flickered on and off. "Occasionally we lose power in here. If that happens, don't be alarmed. They usually have it fixed within an hour or so. As I said, my name is Mary. If you have any questions during this tour feel free to ask. I must tell you, DO NOT touch any of the walls or formations in here. These formations take thousands of years to form, and I wouldn't want to hurt anyone today. I haven't had to use this in weeks." She tapped the side of her waist, where a knife was sheathed in a leather case. "I want everyone to stay together. If you do become separated from the group, stay where you are and you will be found by the next tour. In the past, there have been people inclined to sneak off on their own and explore other parts of the cave. Extremely vicious attack dogs are let loose in the cave at night to guard against spelunkers. I would not want to be left alone in here after hours. Now, are there any questions before we begin?"

"Why is this cave called Gory Caverns?" asked a young boy, whose parents quickly pulled him close.

"Seventy years ago, when this cave was discovered, piles of bones were found in many of the rooms. Most of the skulls had holes and cracks in them. These people did not die pleasant deaths. It is thought this cave served as an underground torture chamber and prison, where hundreds may have met untimely deaths. Some say you can still hear their screams, echoing in dark, distant corners of the cave."

Two boys in the back of the group whispered to each other. "What a crock. Listen to the stuff she's laying on these people."

"I know. The only dog to walk in this cave is her."

"OK, according to the map, there should be a side passage on the right just around the first bend. The tour will go straight. We head right. That should lead us to the main branch, where most of the cave goes."

Mary led them down the main passage, following the hanging string of lights. At the first intersection the boys disappeared into a side passage. The group continued at a fast pace through several rooms, finally coming to a stop in front of a large formation. Several of the tall men were rubbing their heads and checking for blood.

"I'm sorry if I turned off the lights too soon back there. I hope nobody bumped his head on that low-hanging rock. Now, I am only going to say this once. Below is a stalag-MITE and above is a stalac-TITE. You can remember the difference between them because, if you fall in a cave you MITE get impaled on one of them."

Her flashlight shone on a sharp, glistening limestone spike, rising up several feet from the cave floor.

"If anybody asks me the difference between the two again, I will turn off the lights and disappear, leaving all of you to find your own way out."

You could see the joy in her eyes as she took pride in trying to upset the tourists. It was a game she would play to make the day go by. Her groups always stayed close together, never asked many questions, and never stood around awed by beautiful sights. "Get them in and out as quickly as possible," was her motto. They were just paying trespassers in her mind.

"From this point on, I would not look up. There are hundreds of bats roosting on the ceiling, and they don't stop going to the bathroom when you walk under them. Speaking of the ceiling, we are now three hundred feet underground. If there ever was an earthquake, you would never know what happened. But, if the rocks didn't crush you, the cold would slowly chill your trapped body to a slow death. Now, let us continue deeper into Erebus."

As they approached the most beautiful section of the cave, Mary suddenly stopped and turned quickly toward the group. With her knife out, she walked up to one of the ladies.

"May I please see your hand," she requested.

The woman reluctantly held out her hand. On several of her fingertips were small water droplets, shining in the light.

"I warned you about touching the cave," screamed Mary. "Now you will pay!"

Mary grabbed the woman's hand, and attempted to cut off her fingers. The woman screamed out as she pulled back her hand.

"NOOOO! It's water from the ceiling! It dripped on my face and I wiped it off with my fingers! I swear, I didn't touch the cave!"

The group stood in shock. Too afraid to move. Mary backed up, and put her knife away.

"I don't believe you, but fortunately for you, I didn't see you actually touch the walls, this time. Let this be a lesson for everybody here. Do not touch the cave!"

She turned and smiled to herself at a job well done. It was her way to keep this area from getting damaged, and it had worked so far. At the next intersection she asked the group if they would like to continue or take a shortcut to the exit. The group unanimously agreed they were ready to leave. Around the next bend was another steel door that Mary kindly unlocked, and held open. She smiled and nodded to each person as they passed.

"I hope you have enjoyed the tour. Please come again."

"Another successful tour cut short," she thought to herself. After the last person had passed, she grabbed a phone off the wall, and dialed the upstairs number.

"Hello, Charles, I'll be ready for the next tour in fifteen minutes. Oh . . . and don't feed the dogs today. I want them nice and hungry for tonight. Two spelunkers wandered off from the group. They headed out towards the Northwest Passage."

26

Beginnings

Bill's eyes lit up as Tom walked into the grotto meeting. He greeted his friend excitedly, relieved he was still alive. Tom was known to disappear for days while caving alone.

"Where have you been? I've been worried sick about you all week," said Bill.

"You're not going to believe it, I've made a big discovery. I found a huge room. The biggest I've ever seen!"

"Where? How far away?"

"It's out beyond the Forbidden Zone."

Bill stepped back from his friend with a feared look.

"Are you crazy! No one goes out there. If the Elders found out you'd be stopped from caving forever. They may even report you to the State. And then, who knows what THEY would do to you. I could get in trouble just for knowing you went out there. Promise me you'll never go back."

"Will you just calm down. No one knows but you. Now, let me tell you what I found. It's a two-day journey to an area I call Dome City. I finally found a narrow dome and climbed up into it. I climbed for an hour until I came up into a room. When I looked around I saw nothing and I mean nothing. With my strongest light I couldn't see any walls or a ceiling. It's huge! I was too excited to explore. I wanted to come back and get you."

"It sounds cool, but I'm not going out there. It's not worth it. There is plenty of cave right here to keep me happy."

Quietly, one of the older members of the grotto approached Bill and Tom.

"May I have a word with you two."

His name was Wes. He was one of the founding members of the grotto and quite respected throughout the caving community. Together the three walked to a quiet corner of the room.

"I overheard the conversation you two were having. I know you both have a lot of energy and excitement for exploring, this is good, but I will advise you guys to say away from the Forbidden Zone. That is a dangerous place.

"Have you ever been there?" Tom asked. "Do you know of the room I found?"

"I have never been there, but I have lost many friends who have tried. The room you speak of is just a legend, passed down from many generations."

"I was there! I have seen this room! I swear!"

"There is danger out there. Do not return to that place."

"It wasn't that dangerous I tell you."

"Danger comes in many forms my friend. Knowledge can also be dangerous. And with knowledge comes power. Some things are better left as they are. Do not go back."

"But, this could be the biggest discovery yet for our people."

"Leave that area alone."

With that said, Wes walked back to his chair and sat down. Softly, Tom whispered to Bill, "I ain't falling for all that mysterious stuff. I'm going back to that room this weekend, before old Wes goes there and gets all the glory for finding that place. This is our chance to be famous. I was there. It really exists. I swear! Are you coming with me or not?"

"We have to plan this right," was all Bill answered.

Over the next several days, Bill and Tom gathered together all the gear they would need for their journey. They would return in six days, leaving two days to explore beyond where Tom had ended. Four days later, at midnight, so as not to be seen, they started on their journey.

On the afternoon of the second day they came to the area Tom called Dome City. After some searching, Tom found the dome he had discovered that day. Together they climbed, slowly making their way higher in the narrow fissure. Finally they reached the top and climbed up into the room. There they stood breathless and silent as their lights cut through the darkness, only to find more darkness beyond that. Their boots disappeared in a fine dust that covered the floor.

"What did I tell you. Is this the biggest room you have ever seen?"

"I can't believe it. Where do you think it will end?" asked Bill.

"We'll never know sitting here."

They hiked for hours, following a warm breeze with a fresh smell, looking for walls they would never find. They were the first, after hundreds of years, to once again explore the surface of the earth.